"*I think it was a mistake, bringing you here tonight.*"

Romano continued. "It is not fair. I am not an easy man to be with. Since my wife died, I have preferred to keep my life simple, uncluttered. I like it that way."

"And having someone for dinner makes it cluttered and complicated?" she asked tightly. Claire's face was outwardly calm, but her mind was racing. She had *told* him she had no designs on him, hadn't she? How *dare* he presume she was interested in him and warn her off in that way?

He might be wealthy and powerful, with film-star good looks, but he was everything she despised in a man—a conceited egoist who thought he was God's gift to womankind!

She pitied his late wife, she really did....

Sometimes the perfect marriage is worth waiting for!

Dear Reader,

Wedding bells, orange blossom, blushing brides and dashing grooms...and happy ever after? As we all know, the path of true love often doesn't run smoothly—both before and after the knot is tied. So what makes two people's love for each other special? And why can love survive everything that is thrown at it?

In these two linked books I've explored that very thing—how one couple copes with a tragedy that has the potential to destroy their marriage; and, in the second book, how that same disaster sends out ripples of bitterness and disillusionment toward their friend, tarnishing his view of love until...

Well, read the books and all will be revealed! I've thoroughly enjoyed writing them, and do hope you enjoy reading them.

Love,

Helen Brooks

HELEN BROOKS

Second Marriage

Harlequin Books

TORONTO • NEW YORK • LONDON
AMSTERDAM • PARIS • SYDNEY • HAMBURG
STOCKHOLM • ATHENS • TOKYO • MILAN
MADRID • WARSAW • BUDAPEST • AUCKLAND

ISBN 0-373-11939-9

SECOND MARRIAGE

First North American Publication 1998.

CHAPTER ONE

'OH, HOLD on a moment, Grace, she's just this minute walked in.' As her mother thrust the telephone at her Claire's fine eyebrows arched in enquiry, and in the next breath her mother whispered, 'It's Grace. She sounds…agitated.'

'Grace?' Claire almost snatched the receiver in her haste to talk to her friend, this friend who had endured so much in her twenty-five years of life but was now so happy—or had been the last time she had talked to her a week ago.

Don't let anything be wrong. Please, *please* don't let anything be wrong, she prayed quickly as she heard Grace speak her name. Let the baby be all right, let Grace be all right, let everyone be all right… Grace had lost a baby to cot death some years ago, when the child, a little boy named Paolo, was only six months old, and this was her first pregnancy since that terrible time.

'I'm sorry to hound you the moment you get in from work,' Grace said huskily, the strangeness in her voice emphasised by the miles separating them. 'It's just…I needed to speak to you.'

'What's wrong?' There was something wrong; she knew it now. 'You were going for your scan today, weren't you?'

'Yes, yes—and don't worry, there's nothing wrong with the baby,' the disembodied voice said quickly. 'It's just that it's bab*ies*. Plural,' she added as Claire didn't speak.

'*Twins!*'

'Twins.' Grace's voice was flat.

'But that's wonderful,' Claire responded enthusiastically, 'isn't it?'

'Yes, of course it is.' There was a little more animation in Grace's tone now. 'Donato's over the moon, and I'm pleased—I am, really—but I just feel a bit overwhelmed, I suppose.'

'But that's perfectly understandable,' Claire said softly, her big brown eyes darkening with a mixture of sympathy and concern.

Grace had been brought up in a children's home and had never known the support and unconditional love of a mother, and although she had been very close to her husband's mother, Liliana, almost from the first time she had met her, Liliana had died more than two and a half years ago. It was at times like this that it was reassuring to know that mothers, grandmothers, sisters were all at hand, but Grace had no immediate female family members to encourage her, Claire thought perceptively.

'Claire—' Grace stopped abruptly, and then, after Claire gave a gentle, 'Yes?', continued hesitantly, 'I don't suppose there's any chance you might consider coming out here, is there? To live, I mean?'

'To Italy?' Claire stared across the hall in blank amazement, much to her mother's irritation—she was hovering in the lounge doorway trying to make sense of Claire's end of the conversation.

'It doesn't have to be straight away,' Grace said quickly, 'and it can be for as long or as short a time as you want, but I'd just love to know you'd be around when the babies were born. Oh, I shouldn't have asked you,' she continued in a little rush. 'It's not fair. I told Donato it's not fair—'

'Hang on—hang on a minute,' Claire said slowly as she tried to feel her way in a conversation that had suddenly become extraordinary. 'Are you saying you want me to come out and stay with you on a semi-permanent basis? More than a holiday or a long break?'

'Yes.' The reply was immediate. 'For months, if you could. I'd love to have you here, I really would, and with you having trained as a nanny and everything—' This time the sudden halt was even more abrupt, and Grace's voice was hot with embarrassment when she went on, 'Oh, I'm sorry, Claire. I shouldn't have mentioned that.'

'Don't be silly,' Claire said evenly, 'I'm over all that now. But how would Donato feel about my coming to live with you?'

'It was his suggestion,' Grace said eagerly. 'When we found out it was twins he thought I might need some help in the first few months, and he remembered you saying in the summer you were thinking of changing your job but weren't sure what you wanted to do. He thought you could escape the worst of the English winter out here while you took the time to consider all your options, and we'd pay you for as long as you stayed so you'd have a little nest-egg behind you when you went back—'

'No way,' Claire interrupted firmly. 'If I came it would be as a friend helping out a friend. I had that wonderful holiday with you in the summer, and Donato wouldn't even let me pay for my airfare.'

'Well, we'd see.' Grace clearly wasn't going to put any obstacles in the way of her coming at this early stage of the proceedings. 'But do you think you might consider it, then? You could stay in the main house or with us—whichever you like—and Lorenzo would love to have you around for a while. He did miss you when you went home in September.'

'I missed him.' Claire smiled as she thought of Donato's younger brother, who had just turned thirteen and was an enchanting mix of child and young man, with an infectious sense of fun that matched her own. 'He's a smashing kid.'

'I'd love you to come, Claire,' Grace said again, with

a wistful note in her voice that was meant to charm. 'I've lots of friends out here, good friends, but you're different. I've always felt we should have been sisters.'

'I know what you mean,' said Claire. And she did. The two women had only known each other for a few years, but almost from the first time they had met, when Grace had been estranged from Donato and living in England, the two of them had hit it off in a way that only happened once in a lifetime. Claire had five big, strapping brothers, but no sister, and Grace had filled a void in her life that she hadn't even realised was there.

'You'll think about it, then? Look, here's Donato. He wants a word with you too...'

All that had been eight weeks ago, and now it was the end of January, with the chaos of Christmas long forgotten. She had really left the raw winter chill of England far behind her, Claire thought happily as she emerged from Customs and looked around for Donato who was meeting her.

Her old job as receptionist in a doctors' surgery, the bedlam of a home shared with her parents and the three remaining unmarried brothers, the memories of that awful time before she had met Grace—suddenly it all fell away, and she lifted her face to the mild sunlight streaming in through the plate glass windows of the airport terminal, its golden rays turning her sleek chestnut hair to glowing red silk.

'Miss Wilson?' The voice was cold, as was the face of the tall, dark man staring down at her, despite the polite smile that twisted the finely chiselled lips in a semblance of welcome. 'Miss Claire Wilson?'

'Yes?' She wasn't aware that the dreamy expression of delight had been wiped away, or that her velvety brown eyes were revealing her alarm and vulnerability, but the big man watching her so closely was aware of both, and it caused the chillingly handsome face to harden still further.

'I am Romano Bellini—Donato's brother-in-law?' the heavily accented voice said smoothly. 'He was called away unavoidably on a matter of great urgency this morning, and as he did not want Grace to drive in her condition he asked that I would meet you.'

'He did?' Her voice was a squeak, and she heard it with a burst of self-disgust, but somehow the overpoweringly masculine figure in front of her had robbed her of coherent thought. She had seen a picture of Donato's brother-in-law and best friend, of course, taken some time before his young wife, Donato's only sister, had died, but somehow the dormant image captured on film in no way resembled the flesh-and-blood man standing before her.

'You would perhaps like proof of my identity?' Romano asked quietly as she frantically struggled for words. 'Or you would care to make the phone call to Grace?'

'No, no, it's all right,' she managed at last, her voice breathless. 'I've…I've seen a photo of you. I…I know who you are.'

'This is good.' He smiled the arctic smile again, but for the life of her she couldn't respond in kind—her face, like her thought processes, frozen. 'Then there is no problem, *si*? I, too, have seen the photograph of you, taken with Grace in the summer? I understand you had an enjoyable time in Italy?'

'Yes, yes it was lovely.' Say something, talk back, make conversation, she told herself distractedly as he bent and lifted her two heavy suitcases—which she hadn't been able to manage without a baggage trolley and obliging porters—as though they weighed nothing at all. 'I… Grace is all right? There's nothing wrong?'

'Grace is very well,' he replied smoothly, before inclining his head towards the exit doors and saying, 'Shall we?'

'Oh, yes, of course.' She found herself scuttling along at the side of him as though she were an errant child, and the simile annoyed her.

It wasn't just the austere way he had with him that was so intimidating, she told herself weakly as she glanced up at his handsome profile before stepping out into the mild air beyond the airport building, it was *everything*. His height, the broadness of the hard, masculine shoulders beneath the light jacket he was wearing, the dark, cold, enigmatic good looks, the almost tangible air of ruthlessness that permeated his aura like a black shadow. He was... He was frightening.

Frightening? Immediately her mind acknowledged the word she kicked against it with a force that tightened her soft mouth and tilted her chin. How ridiculous could she be? Frightening indeed! He was Donato's best friend, and a good friend to Grace too, from all she had said in the summer, and he had lost his wife in tragic circumstances two and a half years ago. He was probably still devastated by her death; she had been very beautiful. No, he wasn't frightening. Reserved, perhaps? Withdrawn?

She followed him over to the car, a regal, top-of-the-range BMW that swallowed her huge suitcases with consummate ease, and once inside glanced round at the soft grey velvety upholstery as he walked round to the driver's seat after shutting her door.

Donato's wealth and power had overawed her at first during the previous summer, and it looked as though Romano was of the same ilk, she thought warily as he slid into the car beside her. His clothes certainly weren't the off-the-peg variety, his shoes were hand-made and the gold Rolex on his tanned wrist told its own story.

Talk about born with silver spoons in their mouths, she thought wryly. It was more like diamond-encrusted ones in this part of Italy. What a protected, privileged little world it was—unreal by normal standards.

'Is something wrong?'

She hadn't been aware of his eyes on her, but now, as she came out of her musing, she found the narrowed gaze was fixed on her face and flushed hotly. 'No, of course not,' she said quickly.

He continued to look at her as he turned more fully towards her, sliding his arm along the back of her seat as he twisted his body in the confines of the car. 'No?' he asked softly.

It took every ounce of will-power she possessed, and then some, not to start gabbling madly as the silence lengthened and stretched after she had shaken her head, his eyes holding hers in a way she had never experienced before.

'How old are you?' The fact that his words surprised him as much as her was apparent when he immediately followed them with, '*Scusi*, I had no right to ask such an impertinent question.' He swung back into his seat and brought the slumbering engine to purring life, his face cold and withdrawn and his body language expressing the sort of outrage that might have suggested she was the one at fault.

'It's all right.' She addressed the stony profile cautiously, feeling as though she had inadvertently caught a tiger by the tail and very much out of her depth. 'I'm twenty-four, actually, although I know I don't look it.'

'No, you do not.' He didn't look at her as he spoke, negotiating the big car carefully onto the road, his black eyes narrowed against the sunlight which, although lacking in heat, was of a piercing brightness.

'It's genetic.' She spoke brightly, although the flat comment had been if not exactly insulting then less than complimentary. 'My mother looks years younger than she is in spite of having had six children, so I'm resigned to being a teenager until I'm in my thirties.'

The thick black eyebrows arched in wry acknowledgement of her words but he said nothing, and again she felt as though she had somehow been slighted. What an unpleasant individual! She forced herself to look out of the window, keeping her expression blank, although she couldn't stop the warm colour staining her cheeks pink. What a *very* unpleasant individual.

She recalled the picture of his wife and felt herself shrink still further into her seat. The Italian woman had been beautiful—very beautiful—in a sensual, feline way that was both slinky and sexy and very, very grown-up. He obviously preferred his women voluptuous and sophisticated, she thought tightly, a description which most certainly didn't fit her slight, boyish figure and lack of make-up and adornment. Not that she wanted it to, she added instantly, not at all. Romano Bellini was the type of macho man she found positively distasteful—the sort who had to have something decorative hanging on his arm as a reflection of his own masculinity.

'I understand you worked with Grace when she lived in England?' His voice was polite but uninterested, and it was clear he was making the effort of conversation without having any desire to do so. 'As receptionist at a doctors' surgery, *sì*?'

'Yes.' The reply was a little too clipped in view of the long car journey in front of them, so she modified it with, 'Although we had both actually trained to work with children—a fact we discovered as we got to know each other better.'

'This is so?' He turned to her for one moment, and she felt the jolt of the glittering black gaze right down to her shoes before he concentrated on the road again. 'But you found it was not to your liking?' he asked softly.

'Not really.'

'You do not like children?' he persisted.

'Of course I like children.' She wished this conversation, which was proving difficult for her, were being conducted with some space between them. The close proximity of their bodies in the car was...disturbing, and the expensive, delicious smell of him combined with the overwhelming maleness of the man was making it impossible to think clearly. 'It's just...something happened which made it...awkward to continue,' she said carefully. Awkward? Impossible, more like. Terrifyingly impossible.

'I see.' The rapier-sharp gaze flashed her way again, but she had dropped her head a little, allowing the silky fall of her shoulder-length straight hair to hide her face. 'Well, perhaps when the twins are here and you have had some practice again you may feel like continuing your career,' he said quietly.

'Perhaps.' The tone and the word were dismissive, and she meant them to be. There was no way she was going to discuss any of this with a stranger. She couldn't believe she had said as much as she had already, and she certainly wasn't going to elaborate further.

Five minutes crept by in a silence that could only be called taut, and she was just contemplating breaking the crackling tension with a mundane remark about the beautiful countryside when Romano spoke again, his voice cool and contained. 'I thought we would stop for lunch at a little restaurant I know along the coast. This is acceptable?'

'Lunch?'

If he had suggested something obscene she couldn't have sounded more horrified, and his voice acknowledged his awareness of her consternation as he said, 'You do eat, I take it?'

Yes, she ate—of course she ate, Claire thought weakly, but the thought of having lunch with him, of being *with* him like that, was alarming. They hadn't exactly hit it off—besides which, this invitation to lunch was clearly just part of the fulfilment of his duty to

Donato and Grace as far as he was concerned. 'I...I was expecting to eat with Grace,' she managed after a few more painful seconds, 'and I'm not really hungry.'

'I, on the other hand, am starving.' His voice held a thread of something she couldn't quite place, slightly mocking, dry, with a darkness that made warmth trickle down her backbone, and as he spoke he shifted position slightly, bringing the material of his black trousers taut across his thighs.

Oh, help... She took a deep breath and forced her fluttering pulse to behave. What on earth was the matter with her? She'd been alone in a car with a man before, hadn't she?

Yes, but not this particular man, her mind answered weakly. In fact she'd never met a man like this one before. He was threatening. No, not threatening, frightening. Her first instinct *had* been right, she told herself helplessly. He *was* frightening, and dangerous. Too... male.

'So?'

As the cold voice spoke again she forced her eyes up and away from his body, and tried to bring her thought processes into working order.

'You would not find it too...irksome to spare a few minutes to satisfy my appetite?' Her eyes shot to his face now, but the chiselled features revealed nothing but bland enquiry, and the fact that she had put quite a different meaning on his words from their face value brought her colour surging again. 'I think maybe Grace would expect that I feed you before delivering you safely to her maternal bosom?'

He was laughing at her! At the same time as the realisation washed over her a bolt of anger consumed her nervousness. How dared he? How *dared* he laugh at her? He clearly saw her as some small, pathetic mouse he found it amusing to ridicule, and now she was quite sure he had meant his previous words to be taken two ways.

He had sensed the flustered disquiet he roused in her and was mocking it.

Oh... Her teeth clamped together as another thought hit her. He didn't think she fancied him, did he? That she'd been bowled over by his considerable physical attraction and synthetic wealth and charm? She'd die if he did.

Her eyes narrowed, and suddenly the words were there, and flowing as coolly and bitingly as ever she could have wished. 'Of course you must eat, Signor Bellini,' she said icily, and he glanced at her again, caught by her tone. 'I was merely anxious that Grace shouldn't prepare a meal for me and then find I had already eaten, that's all. I have months ahead of me with Grace and Donato, so time is immaterial today.'

And so are you. She hadn't actually said the words but they hung in the air as clearly as if she had voiced them. She knew it and he knew it.

'How gracious,' he said with a silky smoothness that told her the gauntlet had been acknowledged and accepted. 'Are all English girls so courteous?'

'Oh, I'm sure you could answer that question better than me,' Claire returned sweetly as she glanced with studied casualness out of the car window. 'You must have known many women, English and otherwise, Signor Bellini.'

'Must I?'

'I thought I understood Grace to say your business connections stretch all over Italy and the States?' Claire said with a wide-eyed innocence that didn't fool the man at her side for a moment. 'They must bring you into contact with a great deal of people, surely?'

'My business connections... Ah, yes.' The deep voice was wry, and she didn't like the touch of amusement colouring the dark accent, or the way the undeniable sexiness of the Italian voice made her quiver deep inside. 'My business connections do prove...tiring at times.'

'I'm sure they do.' Her voice was a little more tart than she would have liked; she mustn't let him think he was getting to her, so she moderated her tone as she said, 'But then I'm also sure you enjoy your work.'

'I try, Claire, I do try.'

I bet. An elusively sensual whiff of aftershave touched her nostrils briefly as though to confirm the thought, tightening her lower stomach in a way she could well have done without. But he wouldn't have to try *too* hard. Most women would fall into his lap like ripe peaches the moment those velvety dark eyes looked their way, she thought ruefully. But not this woman. Definitely not this woman.

'Now we have determined what a hard-working man I am, may I ask how...busy you were in England?' he asked in a soft, taunting voice.

'Me? Oh, a doctors' surgery is always pretty hectic,' she said brightly, deliberately ignoring what he was really asking, 'but interesting, which is the main thing. I really couldn't stand a job where I was bored.' She rattled on about the day-to-day routine and many panics for a few minutes, knowing he wasn't in the least interested but hoping to divert further questions, but the moment she paused he seized the opportunity to speak, his voice smoky and cool.

'And is there someone in England waiting patiently for your return?'

'A boyfriend, you mean?' she asked carefully.

'Just so.'

'No,' she said flatly.

'No?' She shook her head and the dark eyes brushed her face again for a moment before he said, 'And you are not going to elaborate further on that...enigmatic statement?'

'Enigmatic?' She forced a laugh that she hoped sounded derisory. 'Hardly.'

'But, yes. When a beautiful young woman of twenty-four speaks so determinedly—'

'I wasn't speaking determinedly, just factually, and you know as well as I do that I am not beautiful, Signor Bellini—'

'Now *that* I have to take issue with.' He interrupted her angry retort swiftly, and before she could say anything more continued, 'And please, no more of the Signor Bellini? It is Romano, as you well know, and if you are going to stay at Casa Pontina for some time it will be more harmonious for everyone if we address each other by the Christian names, *sì*? It will make our relationship appear more civil when we meet.'

'When we meet?' This time the naked dismay in her voice was not met with the amusement it had provoked before, and his tone was icy when he said, 'Donato and Grace are my friends, Claire.'

'I know. I know they are—'

'And one visits one's friends, *sì*? Even in England I would have thought this pleasant pastime was still alive and well?'

'Yes, but—'

'So there will be occasions when we meet, share a meal and so on,' he continued in a clipped, terse voice. 'With Donato and Grace, of course, that is all I meant. I was not—what is the word?—propositioning you.'

'I didn't think for a minute you were,' she said, aghast.

'Good. The air is then clear.' The mercurial change was complete; he had returned to suave, cool playboy again with a swiftness that left her open-mouthed and gasping as the powerful car pulled off the road and through a large flower-bedecked arched opening into a quiet courtyard.

'However...' he turned to her as he cut the engine, a slightly cruel smile curving the firm, distinctly sensual mouth and doing nothing to soften the power of his harsh bone structure '…I meant what I said. You are a beautiful young woman, Claire, as any male with discernment would tell you. I admire beauty, even if it is the most corruptive force known to man, as much as I abhor its potential treachery.'

'Its treachery?' she whispered faintly, unnerved by the stony glitter in the black eyes and aware that in a strange way his remark on her appearance was not complimentary.

'But of course.' A veil came down over the handsome face, and she knew he had made a conscious effort to hide all emotion as he smiled again, his eyes revealing nothing more than warm amusement. 'Beauty is a wonderful lure which nature uses to full advantage, *sì*?

'The belladonna—deadly nightshade—with its fragile mauve flowers and dainty poisonous berries, for example, or hemlock's clusters of exquisite white blooms. And then something as enchanting as the flower-like sea anemone, which attracts fish and other animals to their doom, as does the translucent beauty of the Portuguese man-of-war, whose stinging tentacles beneath its shimmering charm paralyse its prey with deadly accuracy. Nature makes full use of illusion, Claire.'

But he hadn't really been talking about plants and animals, she thought suddenly. She was sure of it.

'Yes, I suppose it does.' She stared into the dark cold face as her mind raced. 'But beauty can be wonderful too—something to be marvelled at, to share, something that lifts the soul of man, like a magnificent sunset for example.'

'But within a short time it has faded and is dead, and one is left with the blackness of the night,' he said quietly. 'Nothing lasts. Nothing is what it seems.'

He was talking about his wife being taken from him so tragically. As realisation dawned she stared at him in consternation, not knowing what to say. Bianca had been breathtakingly, wildly beautiful, and they had only had a few short years together before she had died. He still loved her... 'But memories can be precious things, can't they?' she asked softly. 'The sunset might die but the serenity and peace it gives can still live on.'

'I have not found that to be the case,' he said, with a dismissive coldness that told her this strange and disturbing conversation was at an end. 'Now, shall we?' He indicated the charming honey-coloured building in front of them with a wave of his hand. 'You will find Aldonez has a variety of dishes to suit all appetites, so do not be perturbed if you are not hungry. I think it would be nice to sit outside, *si*? There is a delightful garden at the back of the restaurant.'

He had left the car as he spoke the last words, walking swiftly round the bonnet and helping her to alight with a naturalness that told her his good manners were normal behaviour. She remembered Donato had had the same inherent courtesy when she had stayed with them for her two-week holiday in the summer, treating the female race as a whole with a gentleness and protective regard that was wonderfully refreshing in this modern age. But whereas she had just thought Grace's husband a gentleman, somehow with his best friend the whole procedure took on a seductive quality that was more than a little unsettling.

Romano took her arm as they walked across the cobbled courtyard and into the quaint and colourful little restaurant, and immediately she was aware that he was known to the plump and burly little proprietor, who gave them a welcome that could only be described as rapturous.

The greetings over, of which Claire didn't understand a word, Aldonez led them through the main room and out onto a covered veranda where several tables had been placed to catch the full benefit of the weak sunlight. It was surprisingly warm, the veranda being something of a sun-trap, and once she was seated Claire looked around her appreciatively.

The pretty square garden was small, but the lacy perimeter fence was entwined with luxuriant foliage and sweet-smelling flowers. Small shrubs and bushes were scattered between old stone slabs that paved most of the area, with a large magnolia tree in one corner to provide a spot of shade in the summer. 'From March onwards Aldonez packs tables and chairs on every inch of ground,' Romano said with a distant smile as he watched her absorb her surroundings. 'He knows most of the tourists like to eat alfresco.'

'It's very pretty.' She suddenly felt unbearably shy as she glanced at him over the small table, his startling good looks and arrogant masculinity seemingly enhanced by the intimacy of sharing a meal. On the short journey from the airport she had barely noticed the scenery outside the car, her senses briefly registering the southern earthy charm Naples exuded but most of her conscious thought held by the magnetic pull of the man opposite.

Crazy. She lowered her eyes to the menu Aldonez had placed in front of her a couple of minutes before. Absolutely crazy to allow her senses to be dominated like that—and wouldn't he just love it if he knew how she was thinking? When all was said and done, even if he did still love his wife, he didn't have to be so arrogant, did he? So impossible to communicate with, so abrasive?

'Would you like me to translate?'

'What?' As she raised her head and met the hard gaze she would have given the world to be able to say she spoke fluent Italian, but she didn't, and, infuriating man that he was, he knew it.

The fact that she was forced to acknowledge she had been gazing at the squiggles on the card in front of her without even seeing them didn't help either—but that, at least, he *didn't* know.

'The menu? Would you like me to translate for you?' he asked again, his voice patient but with the kind of long-suffering tone one might adopt with a difficult child.

'That won't be necessary, thank you.' She'd rather walk through coals of fire first. 'I only want a green salad and a long, cold drink,' she said evenly. 'If that's possible.'

'Of course.' He bowed his head slightly, and the movement should have been polite but was definitely sardonic. 'May I suggest a side dish of garlic and butter potatoes with that? It is one of Aldonez's specialities.'

'Thank you.' She nodded her head and wondered how someone so altogether stunning could have inspired such dislike in her. 'Is there a cloakroom here? I'd like to wash my hands...'

'*Sì*, just to the left of the main door. I will show you.'

Once alone in the small stone cloakroom, that boasted one deep-set porcelain bowl of ancient origin and one very modern lavatory in bright yellow, she gazed into the ornate and rather fine mirror above the wash-basin despairingly. This had all gone wrong somehow, badly wrong, and she had been so excited earlier in the day. Large, soulful brown eyes stared seriously back at her as she nipped at her lower lip anxiously, her pale creamy skin a perfect foil for her dark eyes and chestnut hair.

Beautiful! She grimaced at her reflection disbelievingly. What an obvious line, and yet it hadn't been like that, not really. But he couldn't have meant it. She shook her head, causing her silky fine hair to flow in a soft wave across her hot face. She wasn't ugly, she knew that, but she was no beauty either—not like Grace. Men had always turned to take a second and third look at Grace, even though her friend was oblivious to their attention most of the time.

Oh, well... She shrugged, dropping her eyes from the mirror and running her wrists under the cold water tap before splashing her face. She was quite happy with who she was, give or take her hot temper and a few other faults she could have done without, so her looks weren't important one way or the other. But she did wish she hadn't got off to quite such a bad start with Donato's friend. She was here to make Grace's life easier and worry-free as her confinement approached, not to enter into a war with her friend's husband's brother-in-law from day one.

She'd just have to bite her tongue and keep quiet when Romano was about. She raised her head and nodded at herself determinedly. She could do that, couldn't she? She should have done it already, not reacted to him like an indignant hedgehog with prickles at the ready. It *was* kind of him to have come all this way to fetch a virtual stranger, and she hadn't even thanked him properly. It wasn't even as if she had met him before and he was renewing an acquaintance; he had been in America when she had come to Italy in the summer and she had left before he had returned.

Yes, she had behaved badly. She prepared to go back to the table full of good intentions. He might be arrogant and imperious, and more than a little high-handed, but he must have some good points for Grace to rate him so highly, and it wasn't as if she'd see much of him while she was here anyway. She'd thank him nicely for coming to fetch her, smile sweetly regardless of how maddening she found him, and refuse to rise to any provocation, intended or unintended, from now on.

He was as far removed from her humble orbit as the man in the moon anyway, and once he'd safely delivered her at Casa Pontina he'd probably barely notice her on the occasions when he came to visit Donato and Grace.

The last thought should have been comforting, but was instead mildly depressing. Oh, for goodness' sake don't be so pathetic, girl, she told herself irritably, before brushing her hair into gleaming order with hard, stiff strokes that set her scalp tingling, spraying a touch of her favourite perfume on her wrists, and then walking firmly out of the cloakroom, her head high.

CHAPTER TWO

'CLAIRE!' Grace waddled out of the front door, her face beaming and her arms outstretched, and Claire had left the car before Romano could reach her door. The two women gave each other as close a hug as Grace's bulk would allow before Claire drew back and looked at her friend with something akin to amazement on her face.

'You're huge.' It wasn't tactful, but they had always been honest with each other.

'Tell me about it,' Grace said ruefully. 'I can't watch any of those wildlife programmes on TV lately, the sight of hippos plodding around hits too near home!'

'Don't be silly.' They were both laughing helplessly now. 'You're still as beautiful as ever, just...'

'Fat?'

'Mumsy, which is exactly what you are going to be, isn't it? How are you feeling?' Claire asked softly.

'Big, tired, achey...and incredibly happy.'

Grace grinned at her and they hugged again before a cool voice behind Claire said, 'Shall we go into the house? Donato has asked me to make sure you keep your feet up, Grace, until he gets back this evening. You and Claire can gossip all you like once you're sitting down.'

'See how it is?' Grace grimaced at Claire as she tucked her friend's arm in her own and turned towards the house. 'If it isn't Donato or Lorenzo fussing, it's Romano. I'm surrounded by men who think I'm going to break.'

'That's no bad thing.' As they walked up the huge stone steps that led to the ornate studded front door of

Casa Pontina Claire smiled at her friend. 'And now I'm here to add my pennyworth to the nagging.'

'"Nagging"?' As the three of them entered the magnificent hall with its beautifully polished floor and air of timeless graciousness Romano stopped and looked down at the two women. 'What is this "nagging"? This is an English word?'

'I suppose it is.' Grace smiled up at him, and Claire was struck by how open and relaxed his face was as he returned the smile. The austerity had gone, along with the coldness, and the result was devastating. He certainly hadn't smiled at her like that.

He really was something else, Claire thought wryly as she watched and listened to Grace explaining the meaning of the word. Not that she was affected by him, not at all, she assured herself quickly. But, nevertheless, one certainly didn't get many men like him to the pound. Or many women who could match such wealth and power and good looks...women like Bianca. They must have made a stunning couple.

Explanations over, the three of them walked into the imposing drawing room where Cecilia, the robust cook, and Anna and Gina, the two little maids, were waiting to greet her, along with a long, low coffee-table groaning with a selection of sandwiches and cakes. 'I thought you might be peckish. It's some time until dinner, although Romano insisted he would take you to lunch,' Grace said happily. 'Was it nice?'

'Very nice.' Claire didn't elaborate further; she was still mulling over the 'insisted'. Although 'very nice' wasn't really the right description if the truth be known, she thought quietly. When she had returned to the table Aldonez had served their lunch within moments, but such had been her state of unease she could have been eating sawdust for all that the food had registered on her taste-buds.

Not that Romano had been difficult at all, she admitted silently, in fact he had metamorphosed into what could only be termed the perfect escort: witty, charming, but still with that indefinable coolness that made her feel as though he was playing a game, observing her the whole time. It hadn't made for good digestion on her part and she hadn't been able to finish the meal, light though it had been. She was absolutely starving now, she realised suddenly, and she filled the plate one of the maids had handed her and watched the other two chat.

'You're staying for dinner, Romano?' Grace asked as the cook and maids left the room. 'Lorenzo is at a friend's house but Donato is picking him up on his way back,' she added as she half turned to Claire, to include her in the conversation. 'And he left express instructions this morning that he wanted his favourite uncle to be here.'

'Did he indeed?' Romano had removed his beautifully cut jacket before sitting down, and now, as he stretched back in his chair, the movement emphasising the hard, muscled chest under the black silk shirt he was wearing, Claire felt herself almost choke on a mouthful of salmon sandwich. Dynamite. With the same destructive power of that particular explosive for blowing the inexperienced into oblivion! 'Well, I think it is rather up to Claire, do you not agree? This is her first evening here. Perhaps she would prefer to spend it with just the family?'

'You *are* family—'

'Of course I don't mind if you stay—'

The two women had spoken together, and although Grace's subsequent laugh was easy, Claire's was forced. She didn't want him to stay, in fact there was nothing she wanted less, but he knew, and she knew, that she couldn't very well say so.

'That's fine, then—a nice, cosy dinner party with all the people I love most,' Grace said with an air of satisfaction.

Donato and Lorenzo arrived home just after seven o'clock—the former full of apologies for being unable to meet her as arranged. And although Claire made all the right noises she was vitally aware of Romano's sardonic gaze as she said how well he had looked after her, and how nice lunch had been.

'This ''nice'', this is another word you English favour, is it not?' Romano said softly in her ear as she rose to go and see Benito, Lorenzo's parrot, at the boy's request. 'With Grace too, the weather is ''nice'', the meal is ''nice''. I find the word singularly unimaginative.'

'Oh.' She was dismayed to find he had chosen to walk with her through the hall to the back of the house, where Lorenzo's own large sitting room was situated and where Benito resided most of the time. 'What would you prefer me to say, then?'

'The truth?' The dark eyes looked down at her, daring her to respond, even as the man behind the mask asked himself why he was doing this, provoking her, trying to get a reaction. She seemed to have taken an instant dislike to him—well, so what? he thought grimly. She was Grace's friend, over here for a few months to help out, that was all. He didn't have to see her above half a dozen times if he didn't want to.

'Which is?' Claire asked carefully, willing herself with all her heart to keep to the pledge she had made in the cloakroom of the restaurant and not let him get under her skin.

He shrugged slowly, his eyes narrowing, and again the sexual magnetism that was as much a part of the man as breathing had Claire's breath catching in her throat. Did he know the effect he had on women? she thought weakly, before answering herself immediately with a curt, Of *course* he did. How could he not? He must have women throwing themselves at him every day of the week. There wasn't a woman born who wouldn't wonder what it would feel like to be in his arms, to have him make love to her, to have him *want* her. She didn't like where her thoughts were leading and slammed the door shut on her mind before they could continue on such a dangerous path.

The Romano Bellinis of this world and the Claire Wilsons had no meeting point; she knew that. He was one of the beautiful people—rich, powerful, with a little black book that was no doubt bursting at the seams with the names of willing females ready to jump when he clicked his fingers. She had seen such women in the summer, when she had been here and the jet set had been in full residence—elegant, sophisticated beauties with model-like figures and dazzling smiles, all legs and teeth and glittering like Christmas trees with the amount of diamonds strewn about their persons. Women like his late wife, in fact.

'Come on, Claire.' Lorenzo, who had been a good few paces in front of them, turned at the door to his room and beckoned to her. 'I told Benito this morning that you were coming and he does not like to be kept waiting.'

She didn't doubt it, Claire thought wryly as she gratefully seized the excuse to finish her conversation with Romano, moving ahead of him as she hurried to Lorenzo's side. Benito was a formidable bird in every sense of the word, but for some reason he had taken to her from the instant his bright, beady eyes had met hers, nuzzling his head, with its wickedly hooked bill, against her fingers whenever she petted him and ruffling his exotic plumage in obvious pleasure at her presence.

It was clear the bird had heard Lorenzo speak her name the second she stepped into the room. His eyes had been fixed on the doorway and the moment he saw her he began to dance clumsily on his perch, screeching her name. 'Claire! Claire! Who's a clever bird, then? Nice old fellow. Nice old bird.' They were the words she had used to pet him in the summer, but she wished

he had said something else, anything else, as she walked
over to him. She could just sense Romano's satisfaction
at his point being emphasised so adroitly.

'Hello, Benito. Who's a clever bird, then?' The big,
compact body was as smooth as silk under her fingers
as she stroked the beautiful feathers, his head immediately nuzzling into her hand as he continued to mutter
his ecstasy at her presence.

'You are not frightened of this old villain?' Romano
joined her, his words slightly disparaging, but as she
glanced up at him, ready to defend the parrot's cause,
she surprised a look of real affection on his face as he
gazed at the bird, before he became aware of her glance
and his expression became blank.

'Benito? Of course not, we're friends—aren't we, old
fellow?' she said quietly, returning her eyes to the parrot,
who glanced up at her cheekily before setting Romano
in his sights.

'Romano...Claire, hmm?' It was said with an air of
consideration that was terribly human, further underlined
by the fact that the irascible old bird glanced from one
to the other enquiringly, like a benevolent matchmaking
uncle. 'Claire e Romano. Nice old fellows...'

'You are getting a little confused, Benito.' Romano's
voice was quite without embarrassment, as though he
had no idea what the bird was getting at—something
Claire hoped fervently wasn't just good manners on his
part. Her own face had turned a vivid and she was sure
unattractive shade of crimson. 'Claire is not a fellow,
nice or otherwise; she is a lady.'

'Lady, lady.' Benito was revelling in the attention he
was getting; he liked nothing more than to show off to
all and sundry. 'Frutta? Frutta?' he asked hopefully,
never one to miss an opportunity to ask for food. 'Nice
old bird,' he added for good measure, giving an imitation
of a heartfelt human sigh as he finished speaking.

'Greedy old bird, more like.' Claire couldn't help

laughing, in spite of her awkwardness, at the bird's roguish manner. She knew all the family were devoted to him—Grace especially crediting him with almost human powers and spoiling him outrageously—and she had to admit that the parrot's mischievous antics and wicked sense of humour were very endearing. But there were times, like a few moments ago, when he was too human for comfort.

'Claire, come and see the new games I had for Christmas for my computer.' Lorenzo saved the day again as he called to her across the room from where he was seated at his desk. 'There is a two-player one,' he added expectantly, augmenting the veiled request with an engaging grin.

'I will leave you to it.' Romano smiled that detached smile as he spoke, turning in the same instant, and as she stood for a moment, watching him leave the room, she found herself reflecting on the power in his male body before she realised what she was doing. A wave of fiery red burnt across her pale skin for the second time in as many minutes, but still the lithe, muscled body under the black silk shirt and casual but expensive black cotton trousers held her attention.

For goodness' sake, had she completely lost reason? she scolded herself as the door closed and she and Lorenzo were alone. She had never in all her life ogled a man, she had never even *wanted* to, and she certainly wasn't going to start now, and with Romano Bellini of all people. He was arrogant enough without her adding to his inflated ego.

Besides which—her mouth tightened as the little voice in her mind spoke with devastating honesty—she could just imagine his reaction to her body if he saw her partly undressed. Her hand made an involuntary protective movement over the flat surface of her stomach before Lorenzo's, 'Come on, Claire, it's all set up,' jerked her out of the brief fall into the black abyss all thoughts of her accident still produced.

Nevertheless, as she battled with Lorenzo for domination of the jungle, her Tyrannosaurus Rex versus his King Kong, her mind was only partly on the game.

It had all been so different before the accident, she thought painfully. She had been happy, confident, content in a job she loved and engaged to a man she was sure was the one and only. And then, in just a few moments of time, her whole life had changed irrevocably. She shut her eyes for a second as a stab of anguish made her heart thud.

It hadn't been her fault. Everyone—the police, her family, the witnesses at the scene—had said the young driver of the flashy sports car had shot out at the junction into the side of her estate car without any warning whatsoever, but the end result had been two grieving parents when he had died in surgery. She had spent weeks in hospital recovering from her own injuries, torturing herself with the terrifying realisation that the three children who had been in the car with her, whom she had been nannying at the time, could so easily have died. As it was, their injuries had been minor, necessitating just an overnight stay, but she could still hear their terror-stricken screams, the moans of the other driver in the tangled wreckage of his vehicle, and the sound of her own voice as she had tried to reassure the children whilst being unable to reach them, trapped as she was within the crumpled car.

She had replayed the incident continuously on the screen of her mind for months afterwards in a desperate effort to reassure herself that she had had no chance to avoid the other car, but still she was left feeling that if she had reacted more quickly, been more observant, a better driver, a young man, eighteen years of age, might not have been wiped out. It had emerged that the sports car had been a present for his eighteenth birthday the day before from over-indulgent and wealthy parents, and that at the time of the accident he hadn't even been wearing a seat belt...

'Claire?' Lorenzo's indignant voice told her she wasn't concentrating, and she made an effort to force her mind from the horrors of the past and into the present.

No one would have been able to prevent the tragedy, given the circumstances that had prevailed, had they been a veteran driver of fifty years' motoring or a young twenty-year-old, as she had been. She knew that, she *knew* it...in her head. Her heart was a different matter. Her heart still had to cope with the feelings of horror and remorse, even though the latter emotion wasn't even pertinent to the incident, according to everyone else. But she felt it. She *felt* it. And her fear and diffidence at being in charge of small precious human beings, who would trust her implicitly the way children do—that was inescapably real too.

The physical scars of the accident might only be faint silvery lines on her stomach, unseen by anyone but herself, but the mental disfiguration was something else, something she knew she had to triumph over, but as yet she was powerless to do so. Would the accident have affected her so adversely if Jeff hadn't deserted her at a time when she had needed him most? Well, she'd never know, would she...?

The death throes of her Tyrannosaurus and Lorenzo's exasperated sigh told her she hadn't been a worthy opponent, and after making her apologies she sat and watched the boy load another game, her mind still worrying at her last thought like a dog with a bone.

Jeff had only visited her in the hospital a handful of times, but, knowing his aversion to illness and disease in general and to hospitals in particular, she hadn't pressured him to come more often—although she had missed him unbearably, and visiting times had become something of a subtle torture as other patients were engulfed by their husbands or boyfriends. Her parents had visited every day, of course, and her brothers and her wide circle of friends had been marvellous. But somehow it hadn't been quite the same.

And then, when she had been in hospital eight weeks, and two days before she was due to come home, she had received the letter, every word of which was imprinted on her mind, on her very soul.

'Dear Claire...' The formality should have warned her of what was to follow. Before then his letters had always begun 'Darling' or 'My precious Claire'.

I don't know quite how to write this letter but I know I must. It wouldn't be fair to either of us if I didn't. This time apart has made me look at our relationship in a new way, has brought certain issues to the fore, if you know what I mean.

No, she hadn't, but she had read on anyway, with her heart pounding so violently it had made her feel sick.

I think it would be better if we had a break, Claire, for six months or so, became free agents again with no commitments. I feel I've tied you down too early and it's far better that we part now than at some time in the future, when we've got children and so on. Please keep the ring and I hope you can understand why I had to do this.

                                        Goodbye. Jeff.

Oh, the hypocrisy of it. But, yes, she had understood then and she did now why he had done it. She was just amazed that she hadn't clicked on to the way his mind was working that first time he had visited her, when the expression on his face as he had looked at her had been one of horror and revulsion at her injuries compounded by a weird sort of panic and disgust.

She had wept, of course, helplessly, hopelessly, for most of the day, and then her eldest brother, Charlie, had come to visit her in the evening and the full truth had come out. It appeared Jeff had been seeing someone else for the last month, a leggy blonde he worked with who was a keep-fit fanatic like him and attended his gym.

'I got those sort of details after I'd hit him,' Charlie had told her, with a measure of satisfaction, 'and if I'm not mistaken he'll need to see a dentist to replace a couple of teeth—unless he picked them up off the pub floor, of course. I was just hoping you'd never have to know about her, sis.'

She had sent the ring back the next day.

'Ready, Claire?' Lorenzo's voice was very long suffering, and she grinned at him, thrusting the memories back under lock and key in that closed room in her mind.

'Ready—and I'm going to paste you this time.'

'You wish!'

She spent just over half an hour with Lorenzo before racing up to the room Anna had shown her to earlier. Her suitcases had been unpacked, her clothes put away in the massive walk-in wardrobe and her toiletries placed neatly in the *en suite* bathroom. It was a beautiful room—the whole house was beautiful, she reflected appreciatively. But she had no time now to gaze out over the sprawling gardens below from the balcony window. She needed to wash away the grime of the day, change into something suitable for dinner and be back downstairs for eight o'clock.

Grace had called by Lorenzo's sitting room ten minutes earlier to say that they were changing for dinner as it was something of an occasion—Claire's first night—that she wanted it to be special and that drinks before dinner would be ready at eight.

At the time it had been a crucial moment in the battle

of the planets—she had been defending Earth against Lorenzo's war probes from Venus—but now she wished she had taken a moment or two to ask Grace how dressy it was going to be. Grace and Donato lived in a massive private wing of the house, which Donato had had built once he and Grace had become engaged, and although access was easy it wasn't quite the same as popping along the corridor to ask advice.

She eyed her clothes, hanging in somewhat meagre splendour at one end of the huge wardrobe, for some precious minutes before realising she couldn't hesitate any longer and quickly pulling the traditional life-saver, a little black dress, from one silk-embossed hanger, teaming it with a pair of elegant black satin court shoes.

After a hasty shower she towelled herself dry with the huge fluffy bath-sheet that smelt of flowers and summer days, and then, with the towel wrapped round her torso, walked through to the bedroom and sat down in front of the long, ornate dressing table.

Should she have her hair up or down? And what about earrings? Little crystal studs or the big gold hoops her parents had bought her for Christmas? And eyeshadow—green or blue? Which would look best? She caught herself abruptly, gazing at her flushed cheeks and sparkling eyes with a little grimace of disgust.

Stop it,—*stop it*, Claire. The words were fierce in her head. He wouldn't look at you twice and you don't want him to. You *don't*. He was married to one stunningly beautiful woman for some years and it's clear he hasn't recovered from her death. If anyone is going to help him forget his pain it isn't a little nobody from England who on top of everything else is damaged goods.

The phrase bit into her consciousness, but it had been with her for the last four years—ever since the day she had read Jeff's letter, in fact. That same terrible evening in the hospital, once Charlie and her parents had left and she was alone, she had remembered Jeff saying the words some months earlier as they had watched a TV documentary on a cancer patient who was getting married after a series of skin grafts.

'How *could* he marry her?' Jeff had been genuinely amazed. 'I mean, she doesn't even look like the girl he once knew. He could have anyone. He doesn't have to have damaged goods.'

'That's awful, Jeff.' She had been horrified, and he had immediately covered his words with an explanation that had deceived her at the time—or maybe it hadn't, she amended painfully. Perhaps she had just believed what she'd wanted to believe, she'd loved him so much. It had taken the accident to show her that the man she had loved had never existed in the first place.

When she walked into the drawing room some ten minutes later, her hair loose and shining like molten copper, and just the merest touch of green eyeshadow her only make-up, Romano Bellini was very still for some moments before walking from where he had been standing, looking out over the dark grounds through the full-length windows, to her side.

'In my country it is mostly the older women who wear black,' he said softly, 'but perhaps it is a tradition that should change.'

'I…thank you—at least I think it was a compliment,' she added, with a disarming uncertainty that made him look at her for one minute more before he threw back his head and laughed—a loud, husky, almost grating laugh, a laugh that sounded as though it hadn't been aired for a long time.

'It was,' he assured her solemnly as she flushed a bright, body-consuming red. 'Indeed it was.'

Claire was aware of Grace and Donato's interested glances from the other side of the room, where Donato was preparing cocktails, and she now felt so flustered and out of her depth that she tried to walk hastily forward, forgetting her unusually high heels, one of which entangled itself in an exquisite Persian rug and would have sent her sprawling but for Romano's firm hand on her arm.

'Steady, little English girl, steady.' His voice was deep and very soft, reaching only her ears. 'I might be the big bad wolf, capable of diverse and terrible crimes, but I am hardly likely to attempt an assault on your virtue in front of my two oldest and dearest friends, am I?'

'Don't be ridiculous. I tripped, that's all.' Her voice wasn't as firm as she would have liked it to be, mainly due to the fact that he had changed from the black shirt and trousers into dinner dress, which, when combined with the midnight-blue silk shirt he was wearing and the wickedly sardonic smile, proved...overwhelming. And stunning. And devastating. She felt the warmth of his hand burning her skin and prayed for calm. This little incident alone confirmed everything she had thought upstairs. They might have come from different planets.

'Of course you did.' His voice was smooth now, and cold, and she felt a sudden and quite absurd disappointment that perversely brought her chin high and made her smile bright as she joined the other two.

Things were a little more comfortable once Lorenzo joined them a few minutes later. She had experienced an immediate rapport with Donato's young brother in the summer, the gift she had with all children as strong as ever, and now they fell into easy conversation as they relived their battles before dinner, teasing each other unmercifully.

'You have a way with children.' As they walked through to the formal dining room at Gina's bidding some minutes later Romano took her arm again, drawing her into his side. 'I can see why your name has barely been off Lorenzo's lips since the summer. He clearly adores you.'

'He's a nice...he's a lovely lad,' she said quietly,

alarmed at the way such a casual touch could make her quiver. 'He's coped with a lot in his short life from what Grace tells me—the loss of his parents and…and his sister,' she continued, after the briefest of pauses when she realised she wasn't being exactly tactful in reminding him of his loss. 'And yet he has come through it all without any bitterness or resentment and emerged as a normal and well-adjusted teenager.'

'Donato and Grace are partly to be praised for that.'

She could smell his aftershave, and whether it was because it was wildly expensive or just that his physical chemistry suited it wonderfully well, the end result was making a sensual warmth tremble deep in her lower stomach as the faint but heady fragrance touched her senses.

'They purposely decided to give the last two or three years to Lorenzo, to make sure he felt loved and wanted for who and what he is, before they tried for a family of their own again.'

'Did they?' She stopped at the door to the dining room, the others having walked ahead. 'They are good people, aren't they?' she said softly as she looked up into his darkly handsome face.

'Yes, they are. But goodness can make one frighteningly vulnerable at times.' His voice was cold now, very cold. 'It is a commodity that is less desirable in this present world than scepticism, I think. To disbelieve, to doubt or question, this is not a bad thing.'

'Not in some circumstances, but you don't mean as a general rule, do you?' she asked, stiffening at the blatant cynicism his words had revealed.

'That is exactly what I mean,' he said expressionlessly, his glittering black eyes noting the indignant flush in her cheeks.

'Well, I don't agree with that!' She glared at him, her eyes honey-gold in the artificial light overhead and her body language militant. 'That's awful. That would mean you could never trust anyone, or believe in them, unless you had a signed affidavit first.'

'A little extreme, but near enough to make no matter.' He gestured to the room beyond with a curt nod of his head. 'I think they are waiting…?'

The dinner table was a vision of heavy, solid silver cutlery, fine crystal glasses, exquisite linenware and a magnificent centrepiece of hot-house blooms that perfumed the air with a sweet fragrance. The room itself was grand and ornate too, and more than a little awe-inspiring, like the rest of Casa Pontina.

As the courses came and went, each one more delicious than the one before, Claire found she didn't have to work at relaxing. Several glasses of good wine combined with Donato and Grace at their best as amusing and congenial hosts were lulling her unease. The tiring day, mostly spent travelling by plane and car, the memories of everything associated with the accident, the confusion and alarm the dark man opposite her evoked—all of it faded into a still, soothing warmth as the wine and good food did its work. It was a calm respite that she knew wouldn't last, but it was wonderfully pleasing on the senses.

They laughed, they joked, they ate and drank, but through it all, every moment, every second, she was vitally aware of the big, dark, laconic figure opposite her, every nerve and sinew tuned into him in a way she had never experienced before. She didn't like it, but there was nothing she could do about it either.

'Did you go home to change?' It was towards the end of the meal that she asked the question that had been at the back of her mind all evening, indicating his immaculate evening wear with a wave of her hand.

'*Sì*, it is not far.' He smiled politely, and his voice reflected his expression as he added, 'You must visit my home at some time while you are here.'

Oh, he didn't think she had been angling for a visit

to his villa, did he? Her calm composure shattered instantly. She hadn't. She *really* hadn't.

'Thank you, but I think I'm going to have plenty to do with the lady in waiting.' She softened the refusal with a careful smile, hoping he would get the message that he was off the hook, but instead of the overt relief she had expected to see in the lethal black eyes his face took on a coolness, a remoteness that was intimidating.

'I am sure there will be an opportunity, nevertheless,' he said stiffly. 'It will be a pleasure to entertain you.'

Brilliant—she'd offended him now. He'd probably guessed she'd sensed he was offering out of courtesy and, with true Italian pride and hospitality, would now force the issue in spite of his feelings just to save face.

'Yes, perhaps. But Donato and Grace have mentioned how busy you are. We'll have to see...' Her voice trailed off as his sombre gaze took hers and held it in a grip that was paralysing.

'Saturday evening,' he said grimly.

'What?' She was aware that the other three had paused in the easy conversation they had been holding about future names for the babies, and that Donato and Grace at least were listening with some interest.

'Dinner at my home on Saturday evening.' It was said without the slightest pretence at an invitation. In fact the cool, harsh words carried more of a challenge than anything else, and it was one she had no intention of taking up.

'I don't think—'

'Donato and Grace too, of course.' There was a cold arrogance in the way he spoke that suggested he knew she wouldn't dare accept an invitation by herself, but even that overt mockery wasn't going to provoke her into agreeing to go to his home, she thought angrily, bristling in spite of herself. Who did he think he was anyway? Ordering her about as though she were some sort of stupid schoolgirl who wouldn't say boo to a goose?

'I'm sorry, Romano. It's very kind of you, but I really would like a few days to acclimatise and get used to things,' she said firmly. 'I'm sure there will be other opportunities—'

'A week on Saturday, then,' he said immediately.

She knew a moment's sheer panic at the fact that a will far stronger than hers was meeting her head-on, and then decided that she had made her point and that to refuse again would be both petty and rude.

'That will give you enough time to…adjust?' he asked with deceptive smoothness, one black eyebrow quirking in a manner that could only be called goading.

'I should think so.'

She managed a bright smile, as though all the undercurrents had completely passed her by, but then stiffened when in the next instant Donato said, 'That would work out very well, in actual fact. Grace and I have tickets for the opera on that night—you remember you bought them for my birthday, Romano? I was going to suggest that Grace and Claire used them instead, but if Claire is happy to have dinner with you we will know she is being looked after, and we could all go to the opera together another time.'

'Of course, a week on Saturday is your birthday.' There was something, just something in the silky soft voice that told Claire that Romano hadn't forgotten the date of Donato's birthday for a moment, or the treat he had arranged for his friend and his wife, and as she turned her head again to look him straight in the eye the black gaze was waiting for her. 'I'm sure Claire would rather you and Grace enjoy the opera together,' he continued pleasantly. 'Is that not so, Claire?'

'I…' Game, set and match! Why, oh why, hadn't she agreed to this Saturday, when Donato and Grace could have come with her? 'Yes, of course,' she said hastily as the black eyebrow rose still further at her hesitation. 'There is no way I would dream of taking your ticket, Donato, you know that, but perhaps the week after that would do just as well?'

'Nonsense.' Romano's voice was brisk now, signalling the end to a conversation he clearly considered had gone on long enough. 'Donato and Grace will enjoy their evening all the more, knowing you are safe in my hands, Claire.'

The black eyes were wicked as they held hers, the message contained in the words for her ears alone, and then his face took on a benevolent expression that made her want to kick him as he turned to face the others. 'That is settled, then, *sì*? A pleasant evening for all concerned, I am sure.'

I'm not. The words were so loud in her head she was surprised the others hadn't heard them, but then, as Romano turned back to her, she knew he had, and had to force herself to say, in as normal a tone as she could muster, 'Thank you very much, I'll look forward to it.'

'Good.' He didn't know how near he came to that kick again as he added, in an innocent drawl, 'It will be...nice.'

CHAPTER THREE

THIS was stupid. This was really, really stupid. Claire frowned ferociously at the girl in the mirror as she leant back against the small upholstered dressing table chair. The very last thing in the world she wanted was to have dinner alone with Romano Bellini, so why on earth was she preparing to do just that? She should have pleaded a headache, flu, mental collapse—anything!

She twisted restlessly on the chair, hating the glimmer of panic in her eyes but unable to do anything about it. She hadn't seen him since that first night she had arrived but had been on tenterhooks every time the phone had rung or the doorbell had sounded—until Donato had mentioned casually at dinner on her third night with them that Romano was abroad for a few days on business. 'He returns Friday night,' Donato had added, as though to reassure her that the dinner date was still on. 'OK?'

No, no it was not OK, but she couldn't very well say so. Romano had tied her up tighter than a bale of hay, he knew it and she knew it, and the rest of them, to her intense irritation, thought he was merely being friendly and supportive to a stranger in his country.

She sighed, loudly and crossly, before leaning forward again and continuing to put the finishing touches to her make-up. She assumed, considering it would be just the two of them, that smart but casual would be the order of the day, and the long-sleeved waist-length jumper in soft white bobbly wool teamed with an ankle-length skirt in dense black denim seemed to fit the bill.

She had decided to wear her hair up, securing the silky

chestnut strands in a high knot on top of her head and allowing just a few strands about her face and neck to combine with her thick fringe and soften the severe style.

A touch of grey eyeshadow on her eyelids and large gold hoops in her ears and she was ready. She fastened the second earring and gazed at her reflection critically. Not bad, quite passable, but nothing on the lines of the sort of women he was used to, she thought quietly. She and Grace had spent one afternoon browsing through old photo albums, and she had been interested to see Bianca had been as beautiful as a baby and child as she was as an adult—interested and dismayed, if she was honest, she amended weakly.

Not that she was interested in Romano. She wasn't, not at all, but it was slightly disconcerting to be having dinner with a man who favoured tall, voluptuous model-types, as the old photographs of the girlfriends he had had before Bianca had borne evidence to, and who had been married for some years to one of the most gorgeous women she had ever seen.

'Donato and Romano were the original playboys, I think.' Grace had been smiling as she spoke, clearly totally undisturbed by her husband's riotous past before he had met her, as her next words had qualified. 'Before they settled down, that is.'

'Umm.' Claire couldn't drag her eyes away from the dashingly handsome man in the photos, who looked almost boyish compared to now. Still, he had lost his wife, she thought soberly, that would be enough to make any man grow up fast.

'Was he very affected by Bianca's death?' she asked Grace carefully, not really wanting to know the answer but having to enquire just the same. 'It must have been an awful shock to you all.'

'It was.' Claire had noticed before that Grace didn't like to talk about Donato's sister, and reproached herself for not keeping quiet as her friend's face changed. She, of all people, knew how traumatic the results of a bad car crash could be for relatives and friends even if the victim lived, and Bianca hadn't. 'But he coped,' Grace continued quietly. 'We all did. You just have to, don't you?'

'I guess.' Claire nodded soberly, her face sympathetic as she reached across and squeezed Grace's hand for a moment. 'I'm sorry, Grace, I shouldn't have mentioned it. I know you and Bianca weren't close, but being the same age and everything it must have been terribly difficult for you.'

'Claire—' Grace stopped abruptly, her face working as she stared into her eyes for a long moment. 'I... There's something...'

'What's the matter?'

But she had never found out what the matter was because a second later Lorenzo had bounded in, closely followed by Donato, and the moment had been lost.

A discreet knock at her bedroom door brought her out of her reverie, and as she called for her to enter Gina's dark head peered in. '*Scusi, signorina*, but the *signore*, he has arrived.' The little maid beamed at her as though she was imparting wonderful news, and Claire dredged up a suitable response as her heart kicked and then raced like an express train.

He was here. As Gina closed the door, leaving her alone again, Claire shut her eyes tightly for a moment, her hand pressed against her chest. Calm down, calm down—he's just a man, for goodness' sake. There's nothing special about him. Even as the thought took shape she acknowledged its absurdity, the tall, commanding figure that had been there at the forefront of her mind for days suddenly as real as if he were in the room with her.

Wouldn't he just love to know he had affected her like this? She opened her eyes wide, straightening her back and setting her mouth determinedly. But he wouldn't. She'd die first. She didn't understand this physical attraction that had hit her like a ton of bricks, not when it was for a man she didn't really know, didn't want to know and actively disliked. It was humiliating, embarrassing, and without any rhyme or reason, but... her thoughts were her own and he didn't have access to them, thank goodness.

She was going to have dinner with him tonight, act cool and uninterested, and hopefully he wouldn't feel obliged to repeat the exercise, having discharged his duties as friend and member of the family. No problem...

The words mocked her a few minutes later as she walked into the drawing room where Romano was waiting. He was sitting in front of the flickering log fire, his long legs stretched out in idle relaxation and his eyes on one of Donato's car magazines which he was idly glancing through, but at her entrance he slowly lifted his head, his expression unreadable as he saw her in the doorway.

'*Ciao*, Claire.'

He was every bit as devastating as she remembered, the black waist-length leather jacket and black jeans emphasising the dark, magnetic power of the man to such an extent that she had to swallow twice before she could say, 'Good evening, Romano.'

'That remains to be seen.' The dark, glossy head tilted with a mocking smile, but such was the look on her face that for the second time in their acquaintance the harsh, husky laugh followed, before he said, 'I apologise, I am being very rude, but you are so good to tease, you know this? Those big golden-brown eyes look at me as though I am the devil himself, and I find it prompts all sorts of bad thoughts. But do not fear, *mia piccola*, I will not ravish you in my lair.'

'No, you won't,' she agreed bitingly, bitterly resenting the implication that she was some nervous, naïve female with goo-goo eyes and a brain to match. 'You won't get the chance, for one thing.'

'With any other woman I might take that as a subtle incitement, a challenge,' he drawled easily. 'But something tells me you mean every word you say.'

'Dead right,' she agreed sharply.

'So. You are not looking for the good time, the brief Italian romance to carry home with you when you go back to England, *si*? This is good. Now we both know where we stand, do we not?' It was said with that smooth assurance he was so good at, but there was the merest inflexion in the velvet voice that told her he wasn't quite so pleased as he seemed.

So the dynamic Romano Bellini didn't like being told exactly how things were by a mere slip of an English girl he wouldn't normally look at twice? she thought perceptively, a warm glow of satisfaction making her lower her eyes quickly before it was reflected in her expression. Tough.

'Shall we go?' She kept her face and voice bland as she raised her head and looked at him again, but then her eyes were caught and held by the magnetic power that was so completely natural and all the more lethal because of it.

'But of course.' He rose with animal-like grace, and in spite of all her determination to remain cool and calm her heart thudded crazily as he walked over to her. 'Here, let me.'

He took her jacket from her unresisting fingers and helped her in to it with an easy charm that was seductive in itself, turning her round with a light touch on her shoulders once she was ready and looking down at her with a strange expression softening the hard, handsome features.

'I hope you will enjoy visiting my home, Claire,' he said quietly, all mockery and amusement gone from his face, 'and that our evening together will be an enjoyable one. You are a guest in Donato's home, but more than that you are a dear friend of Grace's, and as such I would like us, too, to be friends. You understand this?'

She suddenly found she couldn't quite meet his eyes and didn't know what to say, but after a moment she forced herself to reply in as normal a tone as she could manage. 'I'm sure we will be friends, Romano,' she said brightly, half turning towards the door. 'Donato and Grace look on you as part of the family.'

She had expected him to loosen his hold, but instead she found herself turned round again, and without quite knowing how it had happened she was looking up into his dark face, held within the circle of his arms. '*Si*, this is true,' he said softly, his ebony eyes with their thick black lashes hypnotic as they captured her golden-brown gaze. 'Perhaps I am not quite such a monster as you believe?'

As his head lowered she stood quite still in his arms, and then his warm, firm lips had brushed hers in a fleeting kiss that was repeated on her forehead before he straightened, letting her go and turning away in the same movement.

He was halfway across the room before her senses returned sufficiently for her legs to move, and then she followed him hastily, her head spinning and her nerves pounding. It was the Italian way, she told herself desperately as he stopped and let her precede him through the doorway. Like his impeccable manners, his protective and undeniably charming way with women, it was all part of the Latin culture that was so different from the English way of doing things. An Englishman would shake hands, Italians would kiss; it was just a social habit, *nothing more*.

He had just made it perfectly clear he wanted them to be friends for the sake of harmony with Donato and Grace—he had spelt it out, in fact. The moment of tenderness, the way he had made her feel for a split second, that was nothing, not really. She had to keep a grip on herself. She couldn't misconstrue a friendly gesture as something else just because it had affected her so deeply.

No, it hadn't! As the thought struck she denied it harshly. Of course it hadn't. He just confused her, that was all, disturbed her. It was the different culture, the different way of doing things. That was all it—

'Goodnight, Gina.' Romano's deep, dark voice brought her out of the maelstrom of panic in time for her to realise she had walked straight past the little maid without seeing her.

'Oh, I'm sorry, Gina.' She turned with a warm smile, reaching out and touching the young woman's shoulder. 'I didn't see you there. I've promised Lorenzo I'll see to Benito when I get home, cover him up and so on, so don't worry about him, OK?' Lorenzo was spending the night with a friend, and as always Benito had been his prime concern before he had left the house.

'*Sì, signorina.*' Gina looked relieved. The love-hate relationship between the maids and the indomitable parrot provided much secret amusement for the others in the house. Benito was quite aware they were frightened of him and used the knowledge to his advantage unmercifully.

'You go to bed when you're ready, and tell Anna and Cecilia to do the same. Goodnight.'

'Goodnight, *signorina, signore.*'

As Gina opened the door for them and they stepped into the mild February night the air was cool and moist, and scented with the faint perfume of sleeping vegetation and lemon. It all seemed a million miles away from England, which only that day had been caught in the worst winter blizzards for years. The moon was sailing high in the black expanse above, the whispering darkness punctured by a myriad of stars glittering like diamonds on a bed of velvet.

'What a wonderful night sky.' She spoke without

thinking, her face lifted upwards and her eyes half closed as the magic of the Italian night surrounded her, blanketing her troubled mind for a few precious moments. 'It seems too beautiful to be real, doesn't it?' she said dreamily.

'Far too beautiful,' Romano agreed softly, his gaze on the pure outline of her profile before he continued walking to the red Ferrari, parked at the bottom of the steps, where he opened the passenger door for her to slide inside.

'This isn't the car you used to pick me up from the airport.' As she descended the steps she stared at the gleaming sports car as though it would bite her.

'I have two.' His voice was very dry as he added, 'You do not like it?'

'Oh, no, I like it,' she said hastily. 'It's very—' She stopped the word 'nice' just in time, sensing he would be mortally offended if she applied that particular description to the elegant vehicle. 'Very impressive,' she finished weakly.

'I like cars.' He gestured for her to slide in, which she did with more haste than panache, more than a little thrown by the predatory, prowling look of the vehicle, whose commanding lines and smooth arrogance seemed like an extension of the man himself. 'And this one is beautiful and eager to obey my slightest command— very much like the ideal woman, wouldn't you say?' he added silkily.

Her head shot up as she prepared to do verbal battle, but she caught the gleam of wicked amusement in the dark eyes before he could hide it, and said instead, 'You missed "fast" out of your list of desirable attributes, didn't you? I would have thought that would feature highly on your list of priorities for...cars?'

'Just so,' he drawled, with a wry intonation that told her that her point had been received and understood.

As he slid in beside her Claire suddenly understood

the sensual content of all the advertising for such cars. The thing was a metal aphrodisiac, she thought weakly, glancing sideways at him through her thick silky lashes.

He drove slowly along the wide, curving drive surrounded on either side by the magnificent gardens bursting with tropical trees and shrubs, and once through the large wrought-iron gates waited a moment before pulling out onto the road beyond.

Claire had fallen in love with Sorrento, situated high above the clear blue waters of the Bay of Naples, on her visit in the summer. The majesty of the scenic splendour, the fascinating Italian lanes and alleyways, the pretty piazzas and shops had captured her heart, but now the earthy southern charm of the town passed her by as she concentrated very hard on not letting her feelings show.

Control, control... She repeated the word silently all the way to Romano's villa, willing herself to appear cool and collected as she returned his easy conversation without having any clear memory thereafter of what they had talked about.

Grace had told her that the Bellini villa was situated in the Sant Agnello district of Sorrento, among the vast orange groves Romano's ancestors had planted hundreds of years before, which had been the crux of the Bellini fortune for many years. Now Romano, after his father and grandfather before him, had diversified into many lucrative business interests, which virtually amounted to a small empire of which Romano was sole heir, his parents having died in a yachting accident when Romano was still a teenager.

The full moon in the clear, tranquil sky lit up the night almost like day as the Ferrari approached the gates to the villa, and Claire found herself leaning forward expectantly for her first glimpse of Romano's home. She didn't know quite what to expect—something along the lines of the magnificence of Casa Pontina, she supposed—but then they were through the gates and

Romano brought the car to a standstill in the courtyard at the front of the house.

'Oh, Romano…' The villa was quite different from Casa Pontina's imposing splendour, but in Claire's eyes was much more beautiful, being built more in the low, sprawling style of the old days than with Casa Pontina's regal formality. The noble old walls were painted in soft mellow cream, with trailing bougainvillaea and rich red ivy providing vibrant colour, and the leaded windows and black wrought-iron balconies gave the feel of a more tranquil and graceful time, long since gone.

The Ferrari had nosed round a gently cascading stone fountain which stood in the middle of the courtyard, and Claire was enchanted to see a white dovecot, complete with resident doves, in one corner, which further enhanced the air of timelessness. It was beautiful—beautiful, magical and utterly lovely. And for a moment she could hardly speak.

'You like it?' But he had known she would like it, Romano told himself silently. That was why he had brought her here, wasn't it? To impress her, to let her know he was something more than the heartless philanderer and ruthless businessman she had got him down as. But what was he?

He stared for a moment at Claire's profile in the quiet of the car as she gazed at the house. He didn't know. He didn't know what he was any more, or just what he wanted for the future. But he knew it didn't include commitment or ties or ever again being responsible for someone else. That had all finished one summer's day nearly three years ago.

His thoughts moved him out of the car without waiting for Claire's reply, and as he opened the passenger door and helped her to alight he didn't smile, even when she said, 'Of course I like it, Romano. I should think it's got to be the most perfect place on earth.'

'How you English like to exaggerate.' Now he did

smile, but it was the cool, distant smile with which he had greeted her at the airport, the air of cold reserve very firmly in place.

What had she said? Claire felt the rebuff register in her solar plexus even as a spurt of anger brought her chin high and made her voice firm. 'I don't think so.' She walked past him towards the front door, which was a work of art in itself, the fine old wood carved with hundreds of flowers and leaves, each one perfect in its detail.

The atmosphere was tense as Claire stepped into the house, the interior of which matched the outside in its tranquil charm. The polished golden wood of the floor and plain white-painted walls were relieved by just one or two fine old paintings, pure Italian beauty at its best.

'Come through to the sitting room.' He didn't attempt to touch her as he led her past the open winding staircase and into a long, beautifully furnished room that seemed to stretch the length of the house. One wall of it was mostly glass, with massive French windows in the middle overlooking the carefully lighted garden beyond. 'What would you like to drink?' he asked, his voice in neutral. 'Wine, sherry, something stronger?'

'Have I done something wrong, Romano? Offended you in some way?' she asked quietly.

She hadn't intended to say it but somehow the words had just popped out, and now he stared at her for a long moment before he said, 'What makes you think that?'

'You.' She didn't want to antagonise him. She was going to be in Italy for some time and their paths were going to cross more frequently than she would like, but she was blowed if she was going to endure an evening of treading on eggshells. 'You, actually,' she said bravely.

'Claire—' He stopped abruptly, shaking his head slightly as he looked at her standing so small and defiant in front of him, her eyes wide and golden and trying to hide her apprehension, her mouth betraying the vulnerability she was trying to conceal. 'I think it was a mistake, my bringing you here tonight. It is not fair. I am not an easy man to be with. Since my wife died—' He broke off, indicating for her to be seated, and she obeyed without speaking. 'Since my wife died I have preferred to keep my life simple, uncluttered. I like it that way.'

'And having someone for dinner makes it cluttered and complicated?' she asked tightly, hardly able to believe what she was hearing.

Damn it, she was right. What on earth was he thinking of? Romano asked himself savagely. She had made it quite clear that she wanted as little to do with him as possible—it had been he who had pressurised her into coming here. So what was he doing now? She didn't like him and that suited him fine, just fine, but the least he could do was make the evening enjoyable in the knowledge that it was a definite one-off. He just hadn't reckoned on how seeing her here, in his home, would affect him.

'*Scusi.*' Suddenly, as though with the click of a switch, the charmingly remote, wry, arrogant individual was back, the cool, wealthy businessman with the world at his feet. 'You are quite right, Claire, please forgive me,' he said smoothly. 'And now, that drink? What would you like?'

'Dry white wine, please.' She watched him as he poured the drinks, her face outwardly calm but her mind racing. She had *told* him she had no designs on him, hadn't she? And if that hadn't been a clear warning, stating hands off, she didn't know what was. How dared he? How *dared* he presume she was interested in him and warn her off in that way?

Cool and uninterested, Claire, cool and uninterested. Her earlier resolution returned tenfold, and she forced the hurt and indignation into a recess of her mind to examine later when she was alone, determined she wouldn't allow him to get under her skin. He might be wealthy and powerful, with film star good looks and the sort of home that could have come straight off the pages of a Hollywood magazine, but he was everything she despised in a man: a cold, conceited egotist who thought he was God's gift to womankind. She pitied his late wife, she really did. It must have been hell to live with him—

'Will you excuse me a moment while I see to the dinner?' As his voice cut into her thoughts she suddenly realised he was standing in front of her holding the glass of wine, and she almost knocked it out of his hand in her haste to take it.

'The dinner?' She stared at him vacantly. *He* was seeing to the dinner? But what about the cook...? 'Yes, of course. But isn't there someone...?' Her voice trailed away uncertainly.

'To cook and serve for me?' he asked quietly, a thread of something dark in his voice now. 'No, I am afraid you are quite alone here, Claire. There is no one to chaperon you.'

It wasn't what she had meant, but in view of their earlier conversation she didn't mind at all if he put that interpretation on her words.

'We had a succession of housekeepers and maids when my wife was alive,' he said flatly, 'none of whom lasted more than a few months. My wife was...difficult to please in that department. She tended to compare everyone with the excellent staff at Casa Pontina and find them wanting, and once she had died I really didn't feel like going through it all again. It seemed far simpler to look after myself, with the help of a lady in Sorrento who comes in to clean and launder for a few hours every other day.'

'I see.' She stared at him in astonishment. 'So you can cook, then?' This didn't quite fit the image somehow.

'Perhaps you had better be the judge of that once you have eaten?' he parried smoothly.

'Yes, right...'

Dinner turned out to be excellent. The soup, *risi e bisi*, was home-made Romano assured her with a glitter in his dark eyes when she said how delicious it was. The mixture of rice and new peas cooked with onion, ham and butter in chicken stock and eaten with a fork could have been a meal in itself. The lobster that followed was cooked to perfection and melted in the mouth, the accompanying vegetables were succulent and tasty, and the *arance caramellata*—caramel oranges—another home-made work of art.

OK, so he could cook, Claire thought with a slight touch of despair, the two enormous glasses of flowery white wine she had consumed along with the meal making her head swim slightly as she looked into the dark, handsome face opposite her. So what? It should be compulsory for men anyway!

'Coffee?' Romano's voice was deep and soft and did something indescribable to her hormones. 'Or perhaps you would prefer a glass of grappa?'

'No, thank you, just coffee.' Donato always had grappa served at the end of a meal—a spirit distilled from grapeskins made in Bassano which was alleged to help digestion—but, like Grace, she didn't care for it. 'And that was a lovely meal, Romano. I have to say you are a very good cook.'

'Thank you.' He bowed his head slightly and then his mouth twisted in a crooked smile as he said, 'And you did not like having to say it, did you? It slightly spoils the neat little picture you have tucked away in your brainbox, that of male chauvinist pig, eh? But you will find many Italian men know how to cook, Claire, I am not unique.'

You aren't far off, she thought glumly as she smiled

carefully and hoped he didn't realise she was very slightly tipsy.

He had kept refilling her glass every few minutes throughout the long, leisurely meal, keeping her entertained with amusing light stories that didn't betray for one moment anything of the man beneath the outward shell, and she had drunk far more than she realised. Not enough to betray any intoxication, but just enough to feel slightly mellow and relaxed. And she couldn't afford to feel relaxed around Romano; she needed to keep her wits sharp and her head clear.

'We will have coffee in the sitting room.' He moved her chair back as he spoke so she was forced to rise and accompany him to the room she had first seen, to leave the more formal splendour of the dining room where she had felt things were under control, sitting as they had been on either side of the large polished dining table with plenty of hard wood between them.

'Sit down, Claire.' Quite how he managed it she wasn't sure, but instead of the chair she had aimed for she found herself sitting on one of the richly upholstered divans scattered about the room, and within moments, or so it seemed, he was back with a tray of coffee, the aroma of which perfumed the air deliciously.

She didn't know whether to be furiously outraged or relieved when he seated himself in a chair opposite, placing the tray on a coffee-table which he moved between them. Well, so much for her suspicions that she was about to be seduced in spite of all his fine words, she told herself wryly. That would teach her to keep her imagination under control. He clearly fancied the bust of Venus that stood in one corner of the dining room more than her!

It was as she reached for the cup of coffee he was handing her, her mind only half on what she was doing, that the accident happened, and scalding hot coffee poured all over her legs as the cup tilted crazily and then left the saucer altogether.

The thick denim of her skirt saved her from bad burns, but it was still fiercely hot and hurt like mad, and as she leapt up with a strangled scream, her hands patting frantically at her legs, he was beside her in a second.

'Cold water.'

'What?'

When in the next moment she found herself whisked up into his arms and swiftly carried out of the room and up the stairs, she felt all reason beginning to cloud. The pain was severe, but it wasn't that which was making her head spin—or the wine either, come to that. He had lifted her up as though she were a tiny child, his strength formidable, and now, as he walked quickly to one of the bathrooms, holding her securely against the hard wall of his chest, she could feel his heart thudding against her soft flesh, and the sensual, intoxicating smell of him enveloping her until she knew she wouldn't be able to stand when he placed her on her feet.

'Get that off.'

'What?' She stared at him appalled, shocked out of her thoughts as he sat her in a big cane chair next to the shower which he then turned on to cold, directing the jet of water downwards.

'Your flesh will still be burning. You need to take the heat out of it. Get your skirt off,' he said firmly, 'now.'

'You go out, then.' She stared at him anxiously.

'No way. You've had a shock and you might be unsteady on your feet,' he said impatiently. 'I'm not asking you to strip off, woman, merely to remove your skirt. You will still be decent, with a lot more clothing than if you were on the beach.'

She couldn't. She just couldn't. Her hand instinctively covered the faint silver lines that criss-crossed her flat stomach and she felt panic grip her. The jumper she was wearing only reached her waist, and her tiny bikini briefs covered only the bare essentials. He would see...

'Look, I'll turn my back while you take it off and just stand here so you can call out if you feel faint or something.' He was clearly on the point of losing his temper, as his next words proved. 'I'm not going to leap on you when you are at a disadvantage, damn it, and I promise you I won't come within a foot of your body, *but get under the damn shower*!'

She got under the damn shower, stripping off the skirt as the cold water played over her hot legs, and almost immediately relieved the pain. Unfortunately within moments her top was soaking too, the spray covering it despite the downward pointing jet, and as she stood there, dripping wet and freezing cold, with Romano's back to her but his body still managing to express offended outrage, she was seized by the most absurd desire to laugh. So much for her careful preparations for this night out, she thought ruefully. She was now more like a drowned rat than anything else.

'How long have I got to stand here?' she asked meekly after a few minutes, when her legs and torso had gone completely numb. 'I'm freezing.'

'Ten minutes in all—five minutes more,' he said gruffly. 'Do you think you'll be OK if I go and clear up the mess downstairs?'

'Yes.' She paused a moment and then said, 'I'm...I'm wet all over, I'm afraid. I couldn't borrow a robe or something, could I?'

'No, I shall expect you to go home dripping wet or stark naked,' he said with cutting sarcasm. 'Of course you can borrow a damn robe. There's one in the cupboard in the far corner, along with fresh towels if you need them.'

'Thank you.' In view of her position, she kept her voice meek.

Once he had left she duly waited the requisite five

minutes and then stepped out of the shower and towelled herself dry. Her legs were only faintly pink now, and didn't hurt at all apart from being slightly tender at the very point where the liquid had first hit. After stripping off all her clothes she rummaged in the cupboard, which was stocked with enough towels to supply a leisure centre, finding a huge fluffy towelling robe in dark blue at the very back with a pair of matching towelling slippers that were twice the size of her small feet.

She left the dripping wet clothes in the bottom of the shower for now and padded out onto the landing, her hair still in its high knot on top of her head and the robe trailing on the floor behind her as she made her way downstairs, the voluminous sleeves rolled back several times yet still managing to bury her hands. She had never felt such a fool in her life.

'Hello.' She stood still at the entrance to the sitting room, not sure if he was asleep or merely shutting his eyes, but knowing that the sight of him, spread out in the chair with his long legs stretched out in front of him and his hands behind his head, was certainly getting her circulation in full flow again after the numbing effects of the water.

He opened his eyes slowly, straightening in the chair as he did so, but then his eyes caught and held hers in the way they had done once or twice before, their glittering depths mesmerising. He didn't say a word as he stood up, and neither did she, but as he walked across to her, his steps quiet and controlled like a predatory wild animal, she began to tremble very slightly.

'You are cold.' He had seen the tremors she couldn't hide and mistaken them for the chilling effects of the water, but she still couldn't speak, sensing what was to come but unable to stop it. 'Let me warm you.'

And then she was in his arms, and as she felt the hard, male mouth take hers she knew she had known this would happen from the first moment of meeting him. It had been inevitable, like the tide coming in and going out, the sun setting and the moon rising, spring following winter...

As her hands moved upwards to the broad, muscled shoulders her body curved into him all by itself, and his kiss penetrated the soft contours of her mouth in a way that caused pleasure to shoot like a white-hot flame through her limbs.

He was good. He was too good. He must have had hundreds of women to be able to kiss like this, and he was sophisticated, cosmopolitan. This wouldn't mean a thing to him... The thoughts were there but they couldn't compete with what his hands and mouth were doing to her.

'Claire, Claire, so warm and soft.' He was murmuring against her throat now, his kisses burning her skin and causing desire to mount in her like some unstoppable primeval force that was gathering her up and taking her into a world of wild light and exquisite sensation. 'This is crazy, crazy...'

And then his mouth took possession of hers again, hungry, searching, and she clung to him, returning kiss for kiss with a passion that matched his.

She could feel his arousal now through the thin barrier of clothes that separated their flesh, and she knew she ought to feel frightened, apprehensive of its alien power; she had never allowed Jeff full intimacy, and since he had finished with her she had never looked at another man, but somehow, somehow it was a fierce exultation that gripped her senses. *He wanted her.*

His hands had been moving up and down her body on top of the soft towelling, and now, with a little impatient groan of need, he let them slip inside and brush over her breasts, causing her to quiver with awareness. She could feel her flesh swelling as the sensual exploration continued, but then, just as his hands moved downwards past her waist, the movement caused the belt on the robe to loosen and begin to open.

'*No!*' It was instinctive and fierce, the memory of Jeff's rejection, his disgust and revulsion at her injuries suddenly hot and caustic in her head, and before the robe could open fully and betray her she had jerked away with a violence that spoke of panic and fright, turning to one side and pulling the belt tight round her waist. 'No, I—I don't want this,' she stammered frantically. 'I'm not... I can't do this.'

'It's all right. Shush, it is all right.' As Romano took a step towards her she shrank involuntarily, her arms crossed protectively round her middle now and her face white.

'Don't...don't touch me,' she whispered faintly. 'I want to go back to Casa Pontina, please. I want to go now.'

'Don't look at me like that. I am not going to hurt you, Claire.' His voice was curiously expressionless, as though he was exercising an iron control that was taking every ounce of his will. 'I did not intend for this to happen any more than you did. It was just one of those things.'

'It was not "one of those things".' She had to get away, stop this. He might think she was desirable now but he didn't know, and when he did...

'Claire—'

'I mean it—I don't want this. I don't want you.' She was lashing out in terrified self-protection and fear, hardly aware of what she was saying. 'I'm not like you. I don't have affairs, sleep around—'

'Now just a minute,' he said grimly, his whole countenance darkening. 'What the hell have you been hearing?'

'I want to go back.' How could she have encouraged him to kiss her, touch her so intimately? she asked herself. Where were the standards she had lived by all her life? She had only met the man twice, *twice*, and she had allowed...

Oh, she must have been mad, and she couldn't even say it was her moral principles that had made her draw back in the final analysis. It had been panic—panic and fear that he might notice the scars on her stomach and be repulsed by them after all the raging beauties he had had. What was she turning into? It was the wine—the wine and the accident with the coffee. But even as she grabbed at excuses in her mind she knew she was fooling herself. It wasn't the wine or the incident with the coffee. It was Romano Bellini.

'I asked you a question, little English girl.' His voice was cold now, icy, his eyes jet-black gimlets of stone. 'Who has been filling your mind with stories about the big bad wolf?'

'I... No one...no one's said anything.' Now the physical danger was past the look on his face was frightening her. 'I...I saw the photos.'

'Photos?' he growled tightly. 'What the hell are you talking about? What photos?'

'In the albums.' Oh, this was awful. Why hadn't she kept quiet? All she'd done now was make a bad situation ten times worse, she thought miserably.

'I have never had an excess of patience, and the little I possess is fast running out,' he ground out through clenched teeth. 'Now will you please explain what you mean about photographs? Where are they and of whom?'

'At Grace's.' She took a deep breath—her voice had been humiliatingly shaky—and continued, 'And they are of you and Donato and...women, before you both got married.'

'Before...' His voice trailed away incredulously. 'Let me get this straight, Claire. You see photographs of Donato and I when we are young and you assume I am some sort of sexual deviant, is that it?'

'No—'

'But, yes. I think, yes. You are saying I slept with all the women I dated before I got married, is that it? That I had one affair after another, one-night stands, that I—how do you say it?—put it around, *si*?' His accent was very marked now, his rage making him grind out the words slowly, with a force that was intimidating. 'And possibly you think that once I was single again I reverted to my old habits, like a dog returning to its vomit—'

'I didn't—I didn't say that,' she broke in quickly, the harsh analogy shocking her into speech.

'You do not have to.' He took a deep, shuddering breath, obviously fighting for control, and then said, his voice flat now and almost indifferent, 'If it was not for the fact that you are Grace's friend, and of necessity part of the family for the time you stay in Italy, I would not countenance justifying such accusations with the favour of a reply. However...' he stared at her, his eyes narrowed and as hard as black ice '...you will be around for some time and so I will spell it out for you.

'I was not a virgin when I married Bianca, but neither had I run my love-life like a stallion at a stud farm. OK? And one more thing.' Now the eyes were blazing with a rage that was all-consuming. 'You need have no fear that what happened tonight will ever be repeated—you understand this? It was not planned, it was a momentary thing, a whim.' The scorn and contempt in his face as he slowly looked her over was almost more than she could bear. 'And it was not even particularly enjoyable.'

CHAPTER FOUR

SHE had deserved it. As Claire swam up and down the Olympic-size pool, putting every ounce of energy into the fierce exercise as though trying to purge her mind of everything but the physical, the thought that had haunted her since that dreadful night three weeks ago remained stark and clear. She had deserved those last cutting words Romano had growled at her, but, oh, that didn't make them any easier to swallow.

He had driven her home in a taut, arctic silence, she still ensconced in the massive robe, and she had left the car without a word outside Casa Pontina, watching him roar off down the drive with the sickening feeling that she had just made the biggest fool of herself ever, besides alienating Donato and Grace's best friend.

He had called by several times since then, but she had noticed that he carefully avoided being in the same room as her if he could help it. And although he had been very polite and tactful about it she hadn't been surprised when Grace had spoken to her after his first visit, her face concerned.

'Claire?' They had been sitting in Grace's own sitting room in the wing of the house Donato and Grace had christened Bambina Pontina when Donato had had it built. 'You and Romano didn't have an argument or anything on Saturday night, did you? Everything is all right between you two?'

'Of course.' The last thing she wanted to do was worry Grace at this stage in her pregnancy. 'Everything is fine, Grace, don't worry. I just don't think we are particularly compatible, that's all. We don't have any-

thing in common to talk about—that's probably what
you've sensed.'

'Unlike Signor de'Medici?' Grace responded with a
teasing smile. 'I've noticed you two seem to have hit it
off quite well.'

'Attilio is nice enough,' Claire said quietly, 'and he's
certainly an excellent tutor. How long has he been teach-
ing Lorenzo?'

'Some years. Liliana didn't want him to go away to
school or attend one in the district. Lorenzo was only
five when his father died and apparently he was quite
badly affected at the time. Liliana felt the adjustment of
schoolife on top of that would have been too great a
burden on the child. Attilio was recommended by a
friend of hers and he and Lorenzo liked each other from
the start, so it was arranged he would teach Lorenzo
from eight to two on weekdays. It's been very successful
and he's very good with Lorenzo—and Benito,' she
added wryly. 'Although he did put his foot down about
having lessons in the same room as Benito.'

'I can understand that.' The parrot could be extremely
vocal if he felt he wasn't getting his due share of attention.

'He's very good-looking, isn't he?' Grace remarked
casually, although her eyes narrowed as she waited for
Claire's response.

'I suppose so,' Claire answered vacantly. 'Yes, he's
all right.'

'Just all right,' Grace repeated slowly. 'Oh, well...'

Claire climbed out of the pool now, and stood panting
for a few moments in the cool air. It was the beginning
of March and the day was a pleasant one, the temperature mild and soft, but the sun was still without any real
warmth and the fierce heat of summer had yet to make
an appearance.

She was just reaching for her robe, which she had
placed at the pool's edge, when Lorenzo bounded into

view, closely followed by Attilio. 'Oh, Claire, you aren't going, are you?' Lorenzo said immediately. 'Stay a little longer and have a game with us, please?'

'I don't know...'

'It would be good if you stayed, Claire. I think maybe I shall be in trouble if you don't?' Attilio said lightly. 'This young man has been pestering me for a swim for the last half an hour, knowing you were out here, but I am a hard taskmaster and insisted he finished his work first.'

She smiled uncertainly. Taken at face value there was nothing in the tutor's words to make her feel uneasy, but certainly in the last couple of weeks there had been one or two occasions when she had felt Attilio was attracted to her, and if he *was* feeling that way she didn't want to encourage it by word or action. He was good-looking—very good-looking—with his dark eyes and skin and light brown, almost blond hair, but although she enjoyed his company on a day-to-day level she didn't feel any interest beyond friendship.

Attilio had always been the perfect gentleman, as well as amusing and inoffensive, but he had somehow managed to wind the fact that he was at present unattached into their conversations, along with an outline of his pedigree, his preference for English and American girls, and his longing to settle down, at the age of twenty-nine, with the 'right' girl. There had been several incidents, like today, when he and Lorenzo had sought her out once their day's work was finished, and it just made her feel uncomfortable, knowing, as she did, that there could never be anything between them of a romantic nature.

'Come on, Claire.' Lorenzo decided the matter by the simple expedient of whisking her robe out of her hand and pulling her into the clear blue water, where the weak, watery sun caused the ripples to glitter and fragment into hundreds of tiny shiny waves as he splashed her playfully. 'We are going to have a game of tag and

I will be it, yes?' He eyed her hopefully, smiling the charming smile he was so good at and widening his big brown eyes with their thick lashes until she was forced to capitulate.

'Just a few minutes, then.' In truth she felt happier now she was in the water again. Although the neat black swimming costume she had on concealed all of her torso, the way Attilio had looked at her had made her aware that the wet material clung like a second skin, outlining her small full breasts with their cold roughened tips as though she were naked. 'But you're too good at this.'

'I second that.' Attilio was there beside her, and not for the first time she asked herself why she didn't fancy him. The lean, lithe body was well toned and masculine, his shoulders broad and his limbs muscled, but there was no...spark when she looked at him. She didn't know why; there just wasn't. 'And when you have rid yourself of some of this excess energy we will have a game with the beachball, *si*? The piggy in the middle?'

'And Claire can be the piggy,' Lorenzo shouted after them, his accent giving an endearing lilt to the last word.

'Oh, no, Claire could not be a piggy.' Attilio's voice was soft, and she knew he wasn't attempting to make Lorenzo hear. 'Claire is a dove—a pure, gentle dove.' He was matching her stroke for stroke and her uneasiness intensified.

'I don't think so, Attilio.' She swallowed a mouthful of water and coughed and spluttered a little before she continued, 'My mother knows me better than anyone, and it speaks volumes that her nickname for me, right from a little girl, has been Curly.'

'Curly?' They paused in the middle of the pool and trod water as he said again, 'Curly?' glancing at her straight hair.

'After the rhyme, you know?' He shook his head, his brown skin gleaming like burnished silk. 'It goes like this,' she said lightly. 'There was a little girl, who had a little curl, right in the middle of her forehead. And when she was good she was very, very good, but when she was bad she was horrid.'

'And your mother—she thinks you are horrid?'

He was laughing now, and she laughed back as she said, 'Sometimes—yes, definitely sometimes. Or at least I could be. Like the time I tricked my brothers into the cellar because they had been teasing me and wouldn't tell anyone where I had put the key. My father had to break the door down in the end.'

'This is dreadful. I cannot believe it.'

Lorenzo had joined them now, the race forgotten in this interesting conversation. 'What else? What else did you used to do, Claire?' he asked eagerly.

'Oh, I was a little monster.' She told them one story after another, and after a few minutes their combined laughter was resounding round the pool, the three of them holding each other up amid much splashing and hilarity, so it was all the more of a shock when a deep, cold voice cut into the moment with a biting severity that brought their heads swinging round as though attached by the same wire.

'Claire? You are wanted.'

'Romano.' It was only Lorenzo and Attilio's support that stopped her sinking like a dead weight as she saw the big, powerful figure at the far end of the pool, the sunlight behind him throwing the dark face into shadow. 'Is anything wrong?' she asked quickly.

'Grace is not feeling well.' He didn't actually say it was her fault, but he might as well have. 'I think it would be better if you stopped your romping and came back to the house, you understand?' he said grimly.

'Of course I understand,' she bit back sharply, shrugging off Lorenzo's and Attilio's hands and making immediately for the side with strong, urgent strokes, her heart thudding.

Romano was holding her robe as she reached him, and

as he bent down and reached out his hand to pull her out of the pool she saw his face was as black as thunder, his eyes glittering like polished steel as they sliced into her. 'I thought you had come to Italy to be Grace's companion, her friend,' he said tightly. 'Not to play the fool.'

'I *beg* your pardon?' She refused his hand, pulling herself up by her own efforts and managing to get out in one quite graceful movement, something that registered with satisfaction even through the worry for Grace and the burning hot rage at Romano. 'What did you just say?' she hissed furiously, snatching the robe from him and pulling the belt tight once she had slipped into the thick towelling folds.

'That you are needed back at the house.' He had stepped back a pace, and the metamorphosis she had witnessed several times before had taken place—the cold, handsome face quite expressionless now, the ebony-black eyes narrowed and still as they surveyed her hot face.

'I don't mean that and you know it.' She glared at him angrily while keeping her voice low because of Lorenzo. 'How dare you—?'

'Claire?' As she turned Attilio was making his way across the pool with Lorenzo at his side. 'Would you like me to come back to the house with you?' he asked quietly as he reached the side, holding onto the edge of the pool as he looked up at her, the muscles in his shoulders bulging.

She opened her mouth to decline but Romano was there before her, his face still expressionless but his voice gratingly sharp as he said, 'There is no need for that. Grace needs a little peace and quiet and the company of her friend, that is all. I understand you have been down at the pool some time?' he added to Claire without a change of tone, and when she nodded he continued, 'Then it will not be too much of a sacrifice to return now?'

'Of course not.' He was being deliberately difficult and she was going to hit him in a minute, Claire thought furiously, Lorenzo or no Lorenzo. She had been with Grace all morning, and it had been her friend who had suggested she come down to the pool and have half an hour in the cold clean water to blow the cobwebs away. Knowing Grace as she did, she was sure she had made that perfectly clear to Romano. He didn't like her and he was seizing an excuse to try and make her feel guilty and foolish with his insinuations that she was neglecting Grace. Well, he could go and take a running jump, and there was no need for him to have taken such a high-handed attitude with Attilio either.

She looked down at Attilio now, her last thought making her voice warm and soft as she spoke to the upturned face. 'Thank you, Attilio, but I'm sure everything will be OK.' Her gaze moved to Lorenzo who, clearly unaware of the undercurrents among the adults, had been practising his diving while they spoke. 'It would be better for Lorenzo to have half an hour down here, I think, while I see how things are.'

'Of course.' As Lorenzo surfaced again Attilio tapped his young charge on the shoulder. 'Come on, this is supposed to be an hour of physical exercise, so let's exercise, eh? Twenty lengths of the pool, non-stop.'

'Thanks, Attilio,' Claire said quietly.

As Lorenzo swam off, cutting through the water like a brown missile, Attilio smiled up at her before he moved off. 'Any time.' It was noticeable that the smile did not include Romano, and also that there had been none of the courtesy between the two men that was normally apparent.

'Well? Are you going to stand here gazing after your swain or are you going to come back to the house and care for Grace?' Romano asked coldly, bringing her gaze swinging back to him.

'My *what*?'

He was already turning to walk back, and she fell into step beside him, the top of her head on a level with his shoulders.

'Your swain, admirer, suitor—call it what you will,' he said coolly, his hands thrust deep into his trouser pockets and his black eyes narrowed slits as he stared straight ahead. 'I am not sure of the word you would use in England.'

'The word I would use is "friend", actually, not that it's any of your business.' Her eyes were flashing sparks of fire; she couldn't remember when anyone had made her so mad before. 'And I deeply resent your insinuation that I am neglecting Grace, by the way,' she added vehemently.

'Do you?' It seemed the fiercer she got the more distant and controlled he became. 'Well, strange as it may seem to you, I will not lose too much sleep over that,' he said impassively.

'Oh, good.' The sarcasm was thick and heavy. 'That makes it all OK, then, if you're happy, does it? The great Romano Bellini has spoken—the fount of all knowledge, who, of course, cannot be wrong, has given his opinion, yet again, on something he knows absolutely nothing about—'

'Do not test my patience, Claire.'

'Test your patience?' She swung round in front of him now, forcing him to stop as she glared up into his dark, imperturbable face. 'Don't you dare come that—not with me! You storm down here today, flinging all sorts of accusations about—'

'I most certainly have not,' he bit out grimly.

'Oh, yes, you have. Veiled, maybe, but accusations none the less,' she flashed back angrily. 'I know I was out of order at your home that night, and that I said things I shouldn't have, and I'm not proud of it. But I was—' She stopped abruptly and then forced herself to go on. 'I was out of my depth and I didn't want anything to happen we'd both regret. I should have called a halt long before I did, I know that, but there is still no need for you to carry on this…this hate campaign against me,' she finished passionately. 'You're horrible, cold, cruel and I hate you. I really hate you.'

She evaded his hand as it shot out to grab her, jumping back and then turning and running like the wind towards the house. She heard him call her name, his voice hard and angry, but didn't stop until she reached Casa Pontina, exploding into the house like a small tornado before forcing herself to stand still for a moment and adjust the robe with shaking hands. 'Calm down, calm down,' she told herself tremblingly as she fought for control. 'Grace is going to have the twins here and now if you burst in on her like a demented madwoman.'

She took several deep, long breaths, smoothing her wet hair away from her hot face and combing it with her fingers into some sort of order, and then, knowing Romano must be approaching the house by now, walked quickly along to the drawing room where she found Grace sitting on one of the sofas with her feet up and her eyes closed.

'Romano says you're not feeling too good,' she said anxiously as Grace opened drowsy eyes at her entrance. 'What's wrong?'

'Nothing, I'm fine. Just a few aches and pains, that's all,' Grace said sleepily. 'I told Romano that, but men are so panicky when it comes to pregnancy. Donato is just the same. Here's me, with the equivalent of two live and kicking beachballs stuck in the front of me, and they wonder why my muscles object to the load. There's nothing wrong, Claire, really. You would be the first person I'd call if there was anyway.' She sat up straighter as she saw the relief on Claire's face. 'Why?' she asked, wide awake now. 'What did Romano say?'

'That I ought to come back to the house,' Claire said flatly, sinking down beside Grace as her friend swung her legs down and patted the seat beside her, 'and that you weren't feeling well.'

'Oh, men.' Grace sighed deeply. 'Those two will drive me mad before I'm finished—they've even got Lorenzo looking at me anxiously all the time now. You didn't come back before you were ready, did you?' she added anxiously. 'You know if I ever needed you I'd always send Gina or Anna to fetch you.'

'No, I'd had enough anyway.' Claire smiled as she continued, 'Attilio and Lorenzo had just joined me and they were talking about races and all sorts of things, which sounded a bit too physical for me. Pools are to relax in and lie by, with plenty of magazines and a glass of wine, in my opinion.'

'And mine,' Grace agreed feelingly.

'We were just having a bit of fun when Romano came and called me,' Claire said lightly. 'That's all.'

'Were you?' Grace's eyes narrowed. 'And he said you ought to come back to the house?'

'Yes.' There was something in Grace's voice that caught her attention. 'Why?'

'Oh, nothing.' Grace shrugged easily. 'And do I gather Romano was a bit...stressed?'

'About you? Yes.' Claire nodded as she stood up; she had just heard Romano talking to one of the maids in the hall outside, and now seemed like the perfect time to go and have a shower and get changed. With any luck he'd be gone before she came down again. 'I'll see you a bit later.'

'Yes, OK.' Grace sounded a little preoccupied, and as Claire left the room and Romano entered, the two of them exchanging tight nods, Grace's face was thoughtful. So...sparks were flying unless she was very much mistaken. Interesting, very interesting. She ran a contemplative hand across her swollen stomach and smiled up at Romano as he took a seat opposite her. Yes, very interesting.

*   *   *

When Claire walked back into the drawing room some thirty minutes later, her sleek chestnut hair loose about her shoulders and her slim body encased in old denim jeans and a big baggy jumper that reached almost to her knees, she was annoyed to find Romano was still there. Annoyed and disturbed, she admitted honestly.

She would have liked to be unaffected by him, as he was so obviously unaffected by her, but her treacherous heart had started thudding at the bottom of the stairs when she had heard his deep voice talking to Grace, and although her face was blank and cool as she walked into the room her stomach was a quivering jelly.

'Hello, there.' Grace's face was bright and smiling and her voice was cheerful. 'We were just talking about you, actually. I was in a bit of a quandary but Romano has agreed to help out.'

'Has he?' Claire glanced at him cautiously, not liking the implications of her friend's words. The last person, the *very* last person she would want to help her out was Romano Bellini.

'You know we were all going to see Anna and Alessandro at Amalfi tomorrow—you and Lorenzo and Donato and me?' Grace said sunnily. 'Well, I've been worrying a bit today as I really don't feel like the drive.'

'That's no problem; we don't have to go,' Claire said immediately as an awful suspicion filled her mind.

'But Lorenzo would be *so* disappointed.' Grace's tone was reproachful. 'You know how he enjoys seeing Giuseppe, and it's been ages since they got together—besides which, Anna and Alessandro are looking forward to meeting you. I've told them so much about you.'

Claire managed a weak smile and prayed that Grace's next words wouldn't be what she thought they were going to be. Her prayers fell on deaf ears.

'I know Donato wouldn't go if I was going to stay here, but Romano's free tomorrow and he said he'll be happy to take you and Lorenzo to Amalfi. He was planning a visit to Alessandro's soon anyway.'

What could she say? Sheer panic made her ears buzz and killed her thought processes dead.

'So…if Romano picks you and Lorenzo up about nine tomorrow morning, would that be all right?' Grace said in the sort of tone that wasn't really asking a question. 'You'll love Anna, she's a pet, and Lorenzo is going to stay overnight so you can leave any time you want after lunch.'

'Grace, I really don't think—'

'And then I shan't feel I'm messing everyone's day up,' Grace said plaintively. 'I feel bad enough as it is, lumbering about like ten-ton Tessie, but the thought of being a killjoy as well…'

'Don't be so silly—you know you aren't that.' It was a *fait accompli*, wasn't it? Claire thought numbly. Why, oh, why, hadn't Grace asked her about all this first? And why hadn't she hinted to Grace that she didn't like Romano, that she found him difficult to be with—something, *anything* to have prevented this sort of situation arising?

She hadn't wanted to worry Grace by suggesting that her closest friend didn't get on with her husband's closest friend, that was the main crux of the matter, added to which she had never dreamt, in her wildest dreams, that Grace would organise something like this. Grace wasn't an organiser, she never had been. Until now.

'Does nine suit?' Romano's deep, silky voice was bland, but the dark eyes were wicked as he looked straight at her, the wry twist to his mouth informing her that he was aware of exactly what she was thinking. 'Or perhaps you would prefer to leave a little later?'

'No, nine will be…' She took a deep breath and then ground out, 'That will be fine, thank you.'

'Good, good.' Was she the only one who could hear the smooth mockery in that velvety tone? Claire asked herself incredulously. From the contented and maternal smile on Grace's face, it would appear so. 'Then until tomorrow...' He had stood up as she entered the room, his manners as impeccable as always, and now, as he took her hand and raised it to his lips in polite farewell, she jumped as though she had received an electric shock, snatching her hand away as she took a step backwards.

Mercifully his big frame had hidden her from Grace's sight, but his eyes were lethal as she raised her shocked gaze to his face. She hadn't meant to react like that, she hadn't, but her skin was tingling where his warm firm lips had caressed it, heat sending little jumping sensations up her arm.

And then he had turned, making his goodbyes to Grace in a pleasant, easy tone that told her he was far more adept at hiding his feelings than she was, before leaving the room with swift, purposeful footsteps.

That was a good omen for the next day. She plopped down beside Grace, making her time in the pool her excuse for the weakness in her legs. It was clearly going to be a bundle of laughs. He had been coerced into escorting a female he actively disliked to some old friends for the day, and the very nature of the exercise made it embarrassing for both of them. They were going to have to pretend to get on at least, and although she would have Lorenzo to ease some of the tension on the way there, on the way home it would be just her and Romano. Oh, help...

'I worry about him sometimes.'

'What?' Grace's soft voice had only just penetrated the whirling vortex of her mind, and now she forced herself to concentrate on her friend. 'Sorry, I was miles away. What did you say?'

'Romano.' Grace's beautiful blue eyes were cloudy. 'I worry about him living all alone in that great big house without even a cat or a dog for company. It's too solitary a life, even if—' She stopped abruptly.

'Even if what?' Claire asked curiously, feeling, as she had done more than once when she and Grace were alone, that she didn't know the whole story about Romano. But then, did she want to?

'Even if he wants it that way,' Grace said quietly.

'Perhaps he'll change one day.' Claire tried to be comforting. 'When he meets someone else he can love like Bianca.'

'Bianca?' For a moment Claire thought there had been hostility in Grace's voice, but she told herself she must be mistaken.

'Yes, she was so beautiful, wasn't she? And they hadn't been married many years.' Her heart gave a funny little kick and she suddenly found she couldn't go on.

'Oh, Claire, I wish I could tell you.' Grace looked at her almost desperately. 'But I made a promise.'

'I... You made a promise?' There *was* something more to all this, Claire thought bemusedly, but she couldn't even begin to think what. 'I don't understand.'

'I can't... Oh, forget it. I'm talking out of turn. Please, forget it,' Grace said awkwardly.

'It's forgotten.' Claire smiled, changing the subject to one that never failed these days—that of possible baby names. But even as they talked and laughed over the next hour or two she knew that it wasn't forgotten and, more unsettling still, that Romano Bellini had the power to disturb her more than any other man she had met in her life.

CHAPTER FIVE

'WAS it as bad as you expected?' The dark voice was so soft Claire thought she had misheard for a moment. 'Well?' Romano prompted when she still didn't speak.

They were in his Ferrari travelling back along the coastal road from Amalfi after a very pleasant day with Anna and Alessandro—a day when Romano had been the perfect companion, without a frown or taunt in sight, and a day which she had to admit she had enjoyed every minute of.

'I don't understand what you mean,' she prevaricated carefully. 'I was looking forward to meeting Anna and Alessandro, and to seeing the children. Grace had told me what a darling Emanuele is—'

'I meant being with me.'

Yes, she had known that was what he meant, but she had hoped that the uneasy truce might have continued until she was safely back at Casa Pontina. Here, in the close confines of the powerful car, he was too big, too threatening, too…too much of everything, she concluded weakly. 'I…why do you think I expected that to be bad?' she asked quietly, throwing the ball back into his court.

'Didn't you?' he asked sardonically, the cool black gaze raking over her face for a brief moment before he concentrated on the road again, his mouth set in a wry twist.

'No, not really,' she lied politely, her composure slipping a little as he laughed with husky disbelief.

'Oh, I like this demure little English girl image,' he said mockingly, 'it is more restful than the fire-and-brimstone virago I have grown to expect. I thought it was merely for Anna and Alessandro's benefit, or perhaps so you did not frighten the children—'

'Now just you look here!' He'd done it again. In spite of all her good intentions, he'd got right under her skin—but she just couldn't help it. He was so utterly arrogant.

'*Sì?*' The car swerved off the road and executed a neat emergency stop that brought a fine dust-cloud feathering into the air. '*Sì*, Claire, I am looking.' His voice was very deep now, and soft, and although she wanted to maintain her annoyance it nevertheless caused her toes to curl. 'I have to confess I like to look, that I have been looking a lot today. You are very good to look at—'

'Stop it.' She made the mistake of turning to glare at him, and then froze at the expression in his eyes, her whole being becoming still as the glittering gaze held hers.

He lifted a lazy hand to her face, raising her chin slightly as he slowly bent forward and took her mouth in a warm, coaxing kiss that brought desire pounding through her veins and a delicious dizziness to her senses—a dizziness that had her shutting her eyes and just going with the flow before she realised what she was doing and brought her eyes open with a little snap as she jerked away. 'Don't,' she whispered shakily.

'"Stop it." "Don't",' he mocked softly. 'But your body is saying something quite different, is it not?'

'No, it is not.' She was pressed against her door now, her body half turned to his and her face hot. 'And even if it was, it's just chemistry, physical chemistry. That doesn't mean a thing.'

'And this…chemistry that doesn't mean a thing—you are telling me you have felt it with all your other boy-friends?' he asked silkily. 'That you feel it with Attilio?'

'Attilio?' Was he mad? Was he quite mad? she asked herself incredulously. What on earth had Lorenzo's tutor got to do with this? 'Attilio isn't a boyfriend any more than you are,' she snapped heatedly. 'And my love-life—' or lack of it, she amended silently '—is nothing to do with you.'

'True.' He leant back now, crossing muscled arms across his broad chest, his eyes narrowed. The stance did nothing for her equilibrium, emphasising, as it did, the dark, brooding force that was an intrinsic part of his attractiveness.

'So?' She had waited for a full minute until the silence was too much to bear. 'Are we going home or not?'

'Not.' He turned in his seat and the Ferrari growled into life.

'Not?' Her voice was too shrill, but for the life of her she couldn't moderate it as she squeaked, 'What do you mean, not?'

'I mean I do not want to take you back to Grace and Donato yet,' he said with a curious lack of expression in his voice as he swung the car back onto the road. 'Not until we have had dinner at least.'

'But they're expecting me back,' she said frantically, her face panic-stricken. 'Besides which, I'm not dressed for going out to dinner.' Especially after that kiss, she acknowledged desperately, a kiss that had made her feel wild, excited, tempting her mind into all sorts of forbidden avenues—

'You are dressed perfectly.' The jet-black eyes glanced her way for a moment and she felt their power catch her breath. 'For me, that is.'

'Romano—'

'Just dinner, Claire.' His voice was a soft murmur, caressing, dark. 'You have to eat, as do I, so why not together?'

'But—'

'And I will phone Grace to tell her of our plans, OK?' That hard profile wasn't going to take no for an answer, she knew it, and what could she do apart from throw herself out of the car like some thirties heroine with a villain attacking her virtue? Claire asked herself helplessly. But she didn't want to have dinner with him. She knew it was dangerous, that she was playing with fire, and yet on the other hand...she wanted it more than anything in the world. Oh, this was crazy. *She* was crazy—

'OK?' he persisted softly.

Oh, why not? Why *not*? She knew why not, but it didn't stop her mind from continuing. She had had four years of an uphill battle to come to terms with who and what she was since the accident, to put Jeff's betrayal behind her, to control any bitterness and anger that her life had been ripped apart through no fault of her own, to put the harsh memories of the crash, that surfaced occasionally in nightmares even now, behind her.

She had lost all confidence in herself for a time, had reached the bottom of the pit of despair. But she had clawed her way out of it, day by day, week by week, month by month. And one day she would work with children again, would possibly meet someone. It *would* happen. So she wasn't afraid of having dinner with Romano Bellini, she *wasn't*. She wouldn't let herself be.

He wasn't asking her to go to bed with him—her hand instinctively touched her stomach—he was merely suggesting dinner, and she wanted to eat with him, she acknowledged silently, so why not?

'Why not?' She spoke the words out loud, her voice slightly dazed.

'Why not indeed?' There was a great deal of satisfaction in the deep voice.

And if she had pondered on the sudden rush of adrenalin, the shivery feeling that swept over her from head to toe and caused goose pimples to sprinkle her skin, she might have known why not, but she didn't. She smiled brightly, forcing the breath of chill perspiration dewing her skin away with sheer will-power as she told

herself that she was young, single, and it was the most
normal thing in the world to accept an invitation from a
handsome man for dinner. The most normal thing in the
world…

'Oh, it's lovely. It's a gorgeous place, Romano, but I'm
not dressed for somewhere like this—'

'Nonsense.' His arm was around her waist, his touch
light but firm as he guided her through the archway and
into the *sottoportico*, a little passageway beyond which
a magnificent restaurant could be seen, bathed in light
from a hundred or so tiny lanterns. 'All sorts of people
eat here, from kings to paupers,' he said easily.

Yes, and she knew exactly which category *she'd* fall
into, Claire thought wryly as they walked through the
main doors and into a vast room which was almost me-
dieval in its decor.

She had dressed smartly but simply for the visit to
Anna and Alessandro's home, her plain, long-sleeved
shirt in white silk and tailored jade-green trousers ideal
for that occasion, but not for a formal dinner at an expensive—*very* expensive, if her intuition served her
right, Claire thought desperately—and very select hotel.

A quick glance at the tables scattered round the large,
barrel-ceilinged room told her that most of the women
were in cocktail dresses, although the men's clothes var-
ied from full evening dress to casual open-neck shirts
and trousers. Nevertheless, the ambience suggested culture and class, as had the car park stocked with the sort
of cars that always got a second and third glance.

The waiter who greeted them appeared to know
Romano, but she had been half expecting that, and they
were led to a table for two near the dance floor, but in
an intimate little corner, for which she was really grateful. It gave her a chance to relax and get her bearings
without any interested onlookers, and also to absorb the
atmosphere of the place, which was electric. Diamonds

flashed, waiters glided, the music was soft and low and the clientele very definitely the beautiful people—the ones who never glanced at the price tag on anything.

'Do you come here often?' She realised too late it was the ultimate cliché, but he didn't appear to notice, his eyes searching on her face before their dark depths were veiled.

'Not now.' He looked at her impassively, his voice cool. 'But in the past I used to come often.'

He meant with his wife. She continued to hold his glance without flinching, although she longed to break the hold. Bianca would have fitted in perfectly here. All heads would have turned at their entrance—the exquisitely beautiful woman and the commandingly handsome man. She could just picture it. 'With your wife?' She didn't know what had prompted the words, she really hadn't meant to say them, but they were out, hanging in the air between them like live things.

'*Sì.*' He didn't attempt to prevaricate. 'She…Bianca liked this place.'

'Did she?' The surge of jealousy was so hot and fierce that it shocked her.

'Do you?' His words were flat, almost expressionless, and yet somehow Claire felt there was something more hanging on them than the actual question that had been voiced.

What should she say? Her mind raced in the few seconds before she replied, and then she realised that the truth was the only answer. Simple. She wasn't a Bianca, or a Grace, or anything else but herself. And she liked herself. She hadn't at first, in those first bitter days and weeks after the accident, when she had discovered Jeff had left her and convinced herself she was the most worthless creature on earth, but now? Now she did. She *was* worth something, she realised, the bolt of awareness hitting her between the eyes. She had known it for some time but she just hadn't acknowledged it in the core of her emotions.

'Yes, it's very nice.' She didn't flinch from the word. 'I like unusual places, something with a bit of character, and this must be very old.'

'*Sì.*' His eyes had narrowed but otherwise his face remained quite still.

'But...' She hesitated, and then continued, 'It seems a shame that these sorts of places are made into restaurants and things like that in one way—that we lose a little bit of the true past and reduce it to modern-day living. Do you know what I mean?' she finished uncomfortably. 'The nineties are so frantic most of the time, everything seems geared to wealth and power, and people never stop and assess the true values.'

'You did not tell me you were a philosopher.' It was said lightly, but there was something more there behind the cool words and she stared at him uneasily. 'And what, in your estimation, are the true values, Claire?' he asked quietly, his gaze steady on her flushed face.

The waiter returning with the sparkling pink cocktails Romano had ordered interrupted them, but once they were alone again, the menus in their hands, he looked across at her and said slowly, 'Well?'

'What do I consider true values?' She took a long sip of the delicious drink to combat the quivery feeling in her stomach, the sort of feeling that came with confrontation, and breathed deeply before she said, 'The sort I've been brought up with, I suppose—family life, honesty, contentment—'

'And you think all these people do not have such values?'

'I didn't say that.' She hadn't liked his caustic tone. 'You asked me what my values were and I told you, that's all. I do think that many people seem obsessed with succeeding in this era in which we live, often at the cost of family life and friends. I'm not stupid, I know it's necessary to earn the daily crust and all that, but the spirit of the age seems more…aggressive than that. A woman has to be beautiful, to have a perfect body, the right proportions, and men have to be powerful and wealthy to be respected, to have some street cred. The desire to win at any cost, it's…just everywhere.'

'Umm.' He gazed at her thoughtfully, the black eyes narrowed and gleaming like polished stone. 'You seem a little cynical about your fellow man.'

'I'm not,' she flashed back indignantly. 'I'm certainly not. But I don't see the world through rose-coloured glasses either. Half the world is starving because the other half's governments are too greedy, the rainforests are being destroyed for the same reason, and animals, birds, insects become extinct—and all in the supposed name of progress—' She stopped abruptly as she became aware of his amused speculation.

'What a passionate little thing you are,' he said softly.

'Please don't patronise me, Romano.' It wasn't tactful, and it certainly wasn't the sort of pre-dinner conversation to induce indigestion-free eating, but at that moment she didn't really care. He had asked her how she viewed things and she had told him, and she was blowed if he was going to mock her and get away with it, she thought hotly.

'Is that what you think I am doing?' The amusement died very quickly.

'Yes.' She stared back at him defiantly.

'Then you are wrong,' he said, with a strange, tight grimness that checked more words from her. 'I am not patronising you, Claire, far from it. I envy you. I envy you the ability to care so much, to want to see things changed—'

'But don't you?' she interrupted bewilderedly. 'Surely you must?'

'Must I?' His face was dark and cold now, his voice as thin and deadly as a finely honed blade of steel. 'Why must I? I see nothing in my fellow man to care about. Human nature is rotten from the inside out, and even the veneer of civilisation cannot hide it in the final analysis. Self-love is what drives most people, and it is the only true emotion I know.'

'That's awful.' She stared at him aghast. 'You can't say that.'

'I just did.'

'But you can't mean it,' she objected vehemently. 'What about Grace and Donato? They love each other— *really* love each other, don't they?'

'There is always the exception that proves the rule,' he said darkly.

'The world is full of so-called exceptions, then.' She settled back in her chair, eyeing him angrily. 'My parents, for one. You can't lump the whole human race together and say there is no such thing as real love.'

'And you? Have you ever been in love?' he asked suddenly, his gaze on the soft red sheen of her hair before it slowly moved over her creamy skin to hold her velvety brown eyes with his own.

She stared at him for a full minute, quite unable to answer at first. 'I thought I was once,' she said at last, unaware of how expressive her face had been to the big dark man watching her so closely.

'And now? Do you think you were now, with hindsight?' he persisted softly.

'No.' Her voice was flat.

'So what changed?' he asked quietly. 'You do not accept that your love was an illusion, that it couldn't really last?'

'No.' She twisted in her seat as she spoke. 'That's not it—not really. I realise now...' She shook her head, finding the self-analysis painful with those deadly eyes trained on her face. 'The thing is that Jeff wasn't who I thought he was. He had never been the person I imagined. I don't know if it was me being blind or whether he consciously tried to project a different image—I'm not sure—but I do know that when I found out who he really was I didn't like him.'

'And so you finished with him?'

'No.' She looked him straight in the eyes then, and hers were cloudy with pain. 'He had finished with me some time before that, actually, after I had had an accident and he knew I would be in hospital some time. He...he found someone else.'

He swore very softly, in Italian, but she couldn't doubt the meaning, and then said, 'What a fool he must have been,' as he reached forward over the table and took her hands in his. 'What a blind, stupid fool.'

She was quite still, she didn't even dare breathe, and then he rose slowly to touch her lips with his own, cradling her face in his cupped hands for a moment when he raised his head, one finger stroking the soft, full contours of her lips caressingly before he sat down again and picked up his menu.

She felt totally, utterly shattered by the contact, by the tenderness he had displayed that was so at odds with what she knew of Romano Bellini and the image he projected so ruthlessly.

And she had thought she'd got it wrong with Jeff? she thought numbly as she lowered her head and gazed unseeingly at her own menu. That might have been a mistake but it was minuscule compared to the one she had made about Romano. Because she wasn't just physically attracted to this man, it was more, much more than that—as the brief moment of gentleness had forced her to realise.

She loved him. She loved a man whose love for his dead wife had shut his emotions up in solid ice, who was more complicated than any other human being she had ever met, who was wildly handsome, fabulously rich, and as much out of her grasp as the man in the moon.

'Claire?' She came out of the whirling confusion to the knowledge that the waiter had been standing patiently waiting for her order for some minutes, that she hadn't even seen the dancing black letters on the gilt-embossed menu, and that her brain wouldn't allow her to focus on anything but the awful realisation that she had fallen in love with Romano Bellini. 'What would you like?' Romano prompted quietly.

'I...I don't mind—anything,' she stammered awkwardly.

'Perhaps a pasta dish first?' Romano said helpfully. 'Or rice? They do an excellent risotto here. And we could follow that with the fish dish this restaurant is renowned for. The fish is coated in cream and wine and then baked under a coating of breadcrumbs and served with vegetables or salad.'

'Fine, fine.' She nodded feverishly. 'That sounds lovely.'

It *was* lovely. The restaurant was lovely. The wine was more than lovely. And, in her effort to combat the big black cloud that had settled on top of her head and was pressing her into a state of nightmarish panic, she consumed three enormous glasses of it to help her force down the delicious food that stuck in her throat like dry bread. And then she accepted a large brandy with her coffee.

She hadn't got the faintest idea what they had talked about during the meal but she must have made sense, to Romano at least, as he was his normal cool, urbane self, self-assured and coldly in control of himself and those about him. Whereas she... She was mental, crazy, possessed of a death-wish, she told herself bitterly.

Romano. Romano of all people! And he said he didn't believe in love any more? She could tell him a thing or two, because one thing was for sure; if she could have *chosen* to fall in love with someone he would have been the last person in the world she would have nominated.

But love wasn't like that; it didn't allow one to choose in the same way as deciding on a comfortable pair of shoes or a new hat. No, it hit with all the force and destructive power of a ten-ton truck when one least expected it.

'Would you like to dance?' Several couples had taken the floor as they had eaten their meal, and now, as she finished her coffee and brandy, Romano glanced across at her, his dark gaze unreadable.

And be compared in his mind with the woman who still held his heart? she thought painfully. She just bet Bianca would have danced beautifully. That slim, supple body she had seen in the photographs couldn't have done anything else.

'No, thank you, I...I'm a hopeless dancer—two left feet,' she murmured quietly, her cheeks flaming.

'I doubt that.' To her horror he stood up, reaching out his hand for her across the table and drawing her to her feet. 'I doubt that very much.'

'Romano, I really don't want to.' But the trouble was, she did, and as they walked hand in hand to the edge of the dance floor and he turned and took her in his arms, drawing her close into his dark frame, she knew she was the nearest she'd ever be to heaven on earth.

He nuzzled his chin on the top of her head, the smell and feel of him encompassing her in a delight that was sensual and fierce and very, very painful, and after a few moments he drew back to look down into her face, his own warm and smiling. 'I thought you said you couldn't dance?' he challenged softly.

'I can't.' The smile she returned was the best bit of acting she'd ever done. 'I'm just following you, that's all.' She didn't have to dance. She was floating, skimming the air...

'Was that a veiled compliment?' he asked in mocking surprise. 'Careful, you're slipping. I'm the big, bad wolf, remember, and you, you're Little Red Riding Hood,' he finished softly, touching her silky, shining hair with caressing fingers before pulling her into his chest again.

She couldn't stand this. If anyone had told her it was possible to want someone so badly that to be with them was a physical torture she wouldn't have believed it, but there was a hard, grinding ache in her heart region and a sensual warmth in every nerve and sinew that was tearing her apart. And Bianca had had him for five or six years. Had woken up beside him, laughed with him, shared the little intimacies of marriage that were so precious and private, made love with him in the warmth of long Italian nights...

'Claire...' She heard him breathe her name into the scented silk of her hair as he moulded her against him, and then she felt it, with a tiny shock of blinding pleasure—the arousal he couldn't hide.

He wanted her. She shut her eyes tight for a moment and resisted the impulse to raise her head and search for his hard, uncompromising mouth. He wanted her; his body wanted her. Whatever he still felt for Bianca, whatever his heart said, physically he wanted her very much indeed.

'You are beautiful, do you know that?' His voice was whisper-soft and had the effect of sending heat into every pulse-beat. 'So, so beautiful. Your skin is like cream...'

Cream? She thought of the silver threads on her stomach, faint now but there nevertheless, and felt herself stiffen.

'Do not be frightened.' He had sensed her withdrawal and misunderstood the reason for it, his voice husky now as he put her slightly from him. 'I know how you feel about me, and I am not about to force my attentions on you because this...chemistry that you spoke of has reared its head again.' His voice was rueful and she suddenly hated him for it. She wanted him to be devastated, torn apart like she was. 'Just relax, Claire,' he said thickly. 'We're two adult people—surely we can enjoy each other's company for a few hours with no strings attached?'

What did that mean? She wanted to ask him, but he had drawn her back against him, and being held against that hard, masculine frame drove all lucid thought from her head, bringing the senses of touch and taste and smell blindingly alive.

They were on the dance floor for over an hour and he kissed her more than once, bending his night-black head and teasing her lips until they opened under his, only releasing her mouth when he felt her full submission.

She had known deep inside that he was a sensual man, in spite of the cold façade he presented to the world; it was there in the coal-black eyes and firm sexy mouth, the hard, lean body. But the hour on the dance floor was a revelation on how to make love in a room full of people. His body was doing incredible things to hers, as hers was to him—his arousal hot and fierce against the thin material between them—and when she allowed her thoughts to roam further, and imagine what it would be like if they were alone, it made her feel faint.

When the floor-show began they returned to their seats, and she knew she wouldn't have been able to walk but for the firm, hard hand at her elbow. And although she kept her eyes on the big, buxom female singer, with the voice of an angel and the figure of a traditional Italian *mamma*, she was aware of every tiny movement he made, every move of his hands and turn of his head.

They left the restaurant just after eleven, stepping into a cool, fragrant night that was lit with the ethereal allure of millions of tiny stars and the round glow of a full moon, and as they walked to the Ferrari she knew she was trembling and hoped desperately he couldn't feel it through his hand on her arm. She had never felt so vulnerable in her life—not only because of the physical attraction that was so raw and powerful, but also because he had embedded himself in the very quintessence of her mind.

And he didn't want her at all. Oh, his body might seek to slake the need their nearness had aroused, but that was as far as it went. He was a sensual, passionate man and he had been married for a good number of years. No doubt he had been used to making love regularly before he was married too, she added bitterly as Romano opened the passenger door and she slid inside the beautiful car.

But her as a person? A woman? A real flesh-and-blood human being with problems and desires and the whole hundred per cent that went with any sort of commitment? No, he had made it crystal-clear he wasn't into any of that. And probably, more than probably, if he saw her naked even the desire wouldn't be there. He had been used to perfection and that was hard to compete with—not that she ever could have before the accident, but since…

What, if she was being honest, could she offer a man like him? she asked herself as he walked round the Ferrari's bonnet to the driver's side. He had everything; he'd always had everything. Wealth, power, good looks, and no doubt his marriage had been a bed of roses that would always be measured, even if he was unaware of it, against any other relationship.

'That is an oh, so serious face,' he said easily as he slid into the car, and when she didn't answer he tilted her chin and looked deep into her eyes for a moment before kissing her lightly on the mouth. 'Let's get out of here, shall we?'

Was that it? she asked herself helplessly, not sure if she was relieved or furiously angry, although she suspected the latter. After that hour of seduction, and that was what it had been—she discounted the fact that she had been there every inch of the way—was he just going to drive her home and deliver her to Grace like a missing parcel?

He wasn't. When the car stopped a few moments later in a quiet, secluded pull-in surrounded by wispy trees and bushes, she stared at him as he cut the engine.

'I would like to kiss you, Claire, properly.' He turned to face her in the shadows, the quiet of the night making her feel they were the only two people alive in the world. 'I have wanted to kiss you properly all night.'

What on earth had he been doing in the restaurant if not kissing her properly? she thought bewilderedly. But then she found out.

He leant forward and caught her mouth fiercely, and instantly the need was there, raging, overpoweringly strong, taking control of her thoughts, her mind, in a devouring fire that was quite unstoppable. Her lips opened beneath his and he plundered her mouth, the kiss becoming deeper and deeper until the taste and scent of him spun and whirled in her head.

She twisted closer to him, and she knew her action surprised him, her love for him making her sensitive to every movement and reaction of his body, and then his hands began to move over her body in an agony of desire, his harsh, ragged breathing and hungry mouth firing her passion still more.

She couldn't believe what was happening to her. She had never thought of herself as particularly sensual—in fact she had been able to control herself, and Jeff, with a minimum of effort—but this, this was something quite different. She wanted to belong to him, to drown in him, to get as close as she possibly could.

The need he aroused was consuming, overwhelming, dangerous. And he had spelt out just how dangerous. He hadn't pretended he was in love with her, given her any sort of line, in fact he had been brutally honest from the first moment they had met. And she could feed herself excuses again—the romantic setting, the wine and so on—but when was she going to face the fact that she was a convenient commodity, like a packaged loaf of bread when one was hungry? The voice in her head was like a douche of cold water.

'Romano?' She pulled away violently, her vision blurred and her heart beating frantically. 'I need to...I need to ask you something,' she stammered painfully.

'No, not now.' His hands were powerful and strong, his voice thick and husky as he pulled her against him again.

'Yes, now.' She avoided his searching mouth and said, 'Can this ever mean anything to you? Beyond a brief...relationship, that is?' She had been going to say 'affair' but couldn't bring herself to voice the word, knowing she was on the verge of taking just that, devastating though it would be.

'Claire, what is this?'

'I need to know.' Despite the wild clamour of her heart, the desire to be closer and closer, she found the strength to ask even as she knew the inevitability of his answer.

And then he was still. Perfectly still. And she had her answer.

'I want to go back, Romano.' And she did, back to a time when she didn't know Romano Bellini existed, to a world where the worst thing she had had to deal with was Jeff's desertion, the horror of the accident and the nightmarish months that had followed. Suddenly that all seemed bearable compared with the pain that was consuming her now.

'Claire, I cannot promise you anything, you know this. I thought I had made it clear—'

'*You did.*' Her voice had been savage and she moderated it as she said again, 'Yes, you did. You did. I...this is not your fault, but please, please take me back. I want to go home.'

And the painful childishness of her last words brought

his mouth into a thin white line as he turned, fired the ignition, and drove out onto the main road again without another word.

CHAPTER SIX

THE next few weeks were the most difficult of Claire's life, but she got through them. She was a loving friend, companion and confidante to Grace, as well as a mixture of mother and nurse when the need arose; she was a cheerful sister and playmate for Lorenzo, a reassuring and solid support for Donato, and all the time she felt desperately, hopelessly, utterly miserable.

And she couldn't tell anyone. She rang her mother once a week to keep her informed of how things were, but it wasn't the same as a face-to-face chat, and there was no way she could burden her with the knowledge that her daughter was unhappy while she was hundreds of miles away in a foreign country, so she forced herself to sound bright and cheerful and positive.

Romano had been in the States on business for three weeks following their disastrous dinner date, and had used pressure of work as an excuse to cut his visits to Casa Pontina to the bare minimum on his return. It hurt, but not as much as seeing him did on the rare occasions when they met.

It was following one of these visits, in the middle of April, when Grace was eight and a half months pregnant and absolutely enormous, that Grace spoke to her as they sat together in the warmth of the tranquil evening air, Donato and Lorenzo being occupied in the house working out a program on Lorenzo's computer.

'Donato is worried about Romano,' Grace said quietly as she settled herself more comfortably on the cushioned sun-lounger, shutting her eyes as she leant back against its support. 'He feels there's something wrong.'

'Wrong?' Claire had glanced sharply at her friend, but Grace's face was quiet and relaxed, her eyes still shut, and now Claire relaxed a little as she said again, 'Wrong? What do you mean?'

'I don't know—Donato doesn't know—but Romano has been strange recently, not like himself at all. Oh, I know he isn't the easiest person to get on with, especially since—' Grace stopped abruptly and then continued, 'The last two or three years have been hard, but there's something niggling away at him—or so Donato thinks anyway.'

'Has he tried to talk to Romano about it?' Claire asked carefully.

'Yes, but Romano is very much a law unto himself. He always has been.' Grace sighed heavily and opened her eyes, reaching for the glass of lemonade at her elbow and taking a long swallow before she said, 'Perhaps it's just work? He's always worked hard—with his father dying when he did all the responsibility for their business interests went straight onto Romano's shoulders—but since...since the accident he's immersed himself in work. I suppose it's therapy, in a way.'

'Yes.' Claire's stomach was knotted up but she forced herself to say as naturally as she could, 'It can't be easy, losing someone you love in such circumstances.'

'Someone...? Oh, Bianca. Yes, of course.' Grace glanced at her as she replaced the empty glass on the small table at the side of their loungers. 'He didn't say anything to you, did he? When you went out for dinner that time?' she asked carefully.

'Say anything? About work, you mean?' Claire prevaricated, her heart beginning to thump. This would be quite the wrong time for Grace to find out about her feelings for Romano, and his lack of them for her, with the twins' birth imminent. It was important that she was worry-free and relaxed. 'I don't think so—why?'

'Donato seems to think he's been worse since about

then.' Grace settled back against the cushions again, wincing as she tried to ease her aching back. 'Of course, the States thing didn't help. I understand he had to work hard to pull that contract around due to some mess-up in his office in Naples. Heads rolled, from what Donato said.'

'There you are, then. That's probably it.' Claire felt sorry for the heads that had rolled but relieved that an explanation was to hand. 'It's probably just a passing phase, that's all.' And when she went back to England the phase would be well and truly passed, she thought bitterly. Romano was obviously irritated and annoyed that he couldn't visit his friends with the same ease as before. No doubt he held her personally to blame for his predicament. Perhaps she *was* to blame, at that.

As Grace settled down for a nap Claire's thoughts churned on. She should never have let things get to such a stage as she had that night. She should have called a halt long before she did. He had spelt it out to her weeks before, his attitude to women, commitment and relationships, and she had no one to blame but herself. He had probably thought she was game for a flirtation to while away the weeks till she left Italy and returned home—a little amour, a light intrigue that they would both enjoy. Perhaps he'd had bed in mind, perhaps not, but he certainly hadn't expected to be asked the million-dollar question of where the romance could go.

She twisted miserably in her seat, her cheeks burning as she recalled his stony face on the drive home from the restaurant, and the way she had sat huddled in her seat like a small, crushed child. What a fiasco, what an utter, *utter* fiasco. He was used to dealing with sophisticated, capable career women—women who knew what they wanted and exactly how to get it, who were aware of the score and used it to their own advantage in their dealings with the opposite sex. What must he have thought of her?

She cringed inwardly as she stared blindly over the beautiful landscaped gardens in front of her, the lawns and flowerbeds quiet and scented in the late evening air.

No wonder Donato had sensed something unusual in his friend of late. It was probably a lethal mixture of disgust, scorn and sheer exasperation, and all directed at her.

She was deep in the midst of futile self-recrimination when Donato stepped through the open French doors and walked quietly over to where the two women were sitting. 'She is asleep?' he asked softly as he glanced down at his wife.

'Just a minute or so ago,' Claire answered, just as softly. Grace had been finding sleep difficult in the last few weeks, her bulk preventing her from getting comfortable, and the cat-naps she managed most nights left her tired and pale in the mornings. 'Is something wrong?' she added as she glanced up at his dark face.

'There is a problem. The police have just telephoned.' Donato's gaze didn't leave his wife's face as he spoke. 'It appears that there was a break-in at my offices and two security staff were hurt. The thief, or thieves, knew what they were looking for as they made straight for my office and my private safe.'

'Oh, no.' Claire sat up straighter. 'Was anything of value taken?'

'Not in the way of cash—it has never been a practice of mine to hold large sums of money either at the office or here at home—but there were some papers of a confidential nature that might prove troublesome in the wrong hands,' Donato answered distractedly. 'The police would like me to go and see what, if anything, is missing.'

'You go, then.' Claire smiled up at him as his eyes moved to her. 'I'm here with Grace so everything's all right.'

'I could be some time, and Grace was very uncomfortable at dinner,' Donato said worriedly. 'I do not feel I want to leave her tonight.'

'She's been uncomfortable before, Donato.' Claire found it both amusing and touching that this hard, ruthless business tycoon, who had a reputation for rapier-sharp shrewdness and inexorable authority, had been in a state of quiet agitation for days now, every twinge or ache that Grace experienced throwing him into a mild panic. 'And I'm here. I won't leave her for a minute until you get back, OK? I'll sleep in one of the spare bedrooms in Bambina Pontina if you aren't home before we go to bed.'

'I am sorry, Claire.' He smiled at her ruefully. 'You think I am the fool, eh? The—what does Grace say, now?—ah, yes, the whittler?'

'Of course not.' She grinned back. 'She's precious to you, and the babies are precious, but everything is going to be fine, I promise you. Now you go and sort out what's what and I'll let Grace sleep as long as she wants before we move indoors.'

Once he had gone, albeit reluctantly, Claire sank back on the lounger and reached for a magazine from the pile at the side of her. She wasn't going to think of Romano, *she wasn't*—because it was a sure-fire bet he certainly wasn't thinking of her. OK, so she'd been less than wise that evening, but he hadn't exactly been whiter than white, had he? And his attitude since had been plain...insulting. She nodded fiercely and buried her head in the glossy pages.

He had known exactly what he was doing. Once it was there she worried at the thought, unable to let it go. It had been a calculated assault on her senses from beginning to end, a coldblooded exercise to get what he wanted. It was clear he was an accomplished lover and a brilliant strategist.

The memory of how it had felt to be in his arms swept over her and she shivered helplessly. Yes, definitely ac-

complished, she thought wretchedly. Oh, she *hated* him.
But she didn't. She loved him. And therein lay the root
of all her anguish.

When Grace woke an hour later Claire was still gazing
blindly at the same magazine, but she immediately
roused herself and smiled warmly, as though she hadn't
got a care in the world, as she said, 'Hello, sleepyhead.
Enjoy your nap?'

'Yes, I— Oh—oh, Claire...' A few moments of gasping in air later Grace said, 'I think...I think you'd better
call Donato.'

Claire had sprung to kneel at her friend's side, and
now she was the one who gasped slightly. 'It's not—
they aren't coming?'

'They are.' There was a finality in Grace's voice that
brooked no argument. 'I was dreaming I was having
pains, but I was so exhausted I think I slept through it
anyway. But that last one was a definite ''get your bag
packed''.'

'Grace, Donato isn't here.' Claire explained quickly
and then added hopefully, 'Do you think you can wait
until he gets back?'

'I—'

Again Grace's voice was cut off by a contraction,
clearly more powerful than the one before, and it was
Claire who said, 'No, you can't, can you? I...I'd better
call a taxi. Just try and relax.'

'Not a taxi.' Grace reached out a hand and grasped
her arm as she pulled herself into a sitting position. 'I
need to go to the loo and get my things anyway, and in
that time Romano could be here. Donato would never
forgive me if I didn't call him,' she added ruefully.

'Romano?' She knew Donato would want it.

'Yes, call him, would you, and give Donato's office
a ring to let him know what's happening? You might
get the answering machine but leave a message anyway.
That's all we can do.' Grace's voice was marvellously

matter-of-fact, she had clearly switched into birth mode and wasn't about to be flummoxed by anyone or anything. 'Ring the hospital too, and tell them we're on our way. All the numbers are by the phone in the hall.'

By the time Romano strode through the door, after Claire's terse telephone call of very few words, Grace had just walked through from her own quarters with Lorenzo and Claire at her side and sunk into a chair by the front door.

'You must have driven like a madman,' Grace said blithely, ignoring his frowning dark face as she stood up slowly, Claire holding her elbow. 'There was no need—'

Her voice was cut off, and Claire and Romano took her weight as she leant forward, breathing heavily, as another pain hit. 'They're every six minutes now, so I think there *is* a need,' Claire said grimly, and their eyes met over Grace's red-gold curls. 'I'd get there as fast as possible, if I were you. Now they've decided to be born they can't wait.'

Romano swore, softly but with heartfelt intensity, and then lifted Grace bodily into his arms, beckoning with his head for Claire to open the front door and saying to Lorenzo, 'Hold the fort, OK? You are in charge now. Claire has told you she has left a message for Donato?' Lorenzo nodded, his brown eyes enormous. 'He will probably come straight to the hospital, but if he telephones tell him what is happening—you understand?'

'*Sì.*' Lorenzo's voice was little more than a whisper. 'And...and Grace...?'

'Grace is going to be fine.' Romano's voice was soft now, tender, and it made Claire want to howl as it touched something deep inside. 'Trust me, Lorenzo. All is well, OK?' His dark eyes were steady as they held the boy's gaze. 'You know I would not lie to you?' he said as he let Grace's feet touch the floor again.

'*Sì.*' Lorenzo's voice was a little stronger.

'Then take care of things here—I can ask you to do

this?' Romano asked quietly. 'As soon as there is news you will be the first to know, but for now Donato needs you to take charge so that he can concentrate on Grace and the babies without worrying about home.'

'I can do this.' Lorenzo's voice was suddenly ridiculously like Donato's, and the lump in Claire's throat grew.

'I know.' Romano leant forward, but instead of patting Lorenzo on the head, or ruffling his black curls as he had been wont to do in the past, he held out his hand for the young boy to shake, causing Lorenzo to swell visibly as he solemnly shook his brother-in-law's hand before Romano lifted Grace into his arms again.

He'd handled Lorenzo's nerves perfectly. The thought was at the forefront of Claire's mind as Romano carried Grace, who was now protesting strongly that she was quite capable of walking, out to the BMW, where he deposited her on the back seat and placed a light blanket over her legs. 'Be quiet, woman, and put your mind to your breathing or panting or whatever it is women do at this time,' he said with mock severity, before shutting the car door and indicating for Claire to sit in the front passenger seat.

As the powerful engine purred into life and the car moved smoothly away Claire waved at Lorenzo, who was standing on the steps, until they turned a corner in the long drive and he was lost to view. 'You were very good with him back there.' She spoke the thought that had been on her mind, and Grace added her agreement from the back seat.

'He needed to be given something to do, something to focus his mind on, that is all,' Romano said quietly. 'He is a Vittoria. It is not in his nature to sit around and twiddle his thumbs.'

'It's not in a Bellini's nature either,' Grace piped up again, before a slight groan and some heavy breathing told the two in the front that the conversation was finished.

Once they were at the hospital the medical machine took over, but when Grace was established in a private room a nurse came to tell Claire that she was wanted. 'I understand the husband, he is on his way?' the rotund middle-aged woman asked quietly, with a polite nod at Romano, who was sitting in the small waiting room, legs outstretched and seemingly relaxed. But he wasn't. Claire knew he wasn't. Quite how she knew, she wasn't sure, but this calm, composed air was an act. She *knew* it. 'If your husband does not mind waiting, Signora Vittoria would like to see you.'

'He...I'm not married. This is a friend of Signor Vittoria,' Claire said stiffly, her cheeks flaming. 'You'll wait for Donato?' she added as she turned to face Romano. 'The policeman who was manning the phone at his office was going to find him straight away. He was out somewhere talking to one of the security people, so he shouldn't be long.'

'Of course I will wait,' he said quietly, the dark eyes expressionless as they looked into hers and his aura of cool remoteness sitting on him like a cloak.

How could one man be so...complete? she asked herself painfully as she followed the nurse out of the room and into the gleaming white corridor outside. Didn't he let anything touch him any more? He was so contained, so in control. She had never met anyone who had such command of themselves and their emotions. It wasn't just intimidating, it was frightening.

He wasn't going to be able to take this. Once he was alone Romano sprung up out of his seat, his teeth clenched and his body taut as he strode across to the small, narrow window and stared out into the darkness beyond.

He had dreamt her, breathed her, tasted her for

weeks... It was a physical thing, dammit, it was just a physical thing—and as such could be dealt with. The thought was hot and fierce.

He thrust his hands deep into his pockets, his black leather jacket and black jeans emphasising the dark aura that permeated from the powerful frame like an icy cold cloud.

Why hadn't he gone out and got a woman—any woman—to relieve the ache inside him? he asked himself savagely. There were any number he knew who would be only too willing to fall into his bed, so why hadn't he behaved as she expected him to behave, dammit? She credited him with as little finesse in these matters as a stud stallion, she had made that clear from day one, so why didn't he kill this ridiculous craving in the age-old way? This was a body thing, an annoying and inconvenient irritation. *That was all it was*. He knew it— hell, he knew it in his head, so why didn't his body take notice?

A sudden noise from the corridor outside caught his attention and he swung round to face the door, but when it remained closed he turned back to the darkness outside the window, his thoughts moving off at a tangent now. He should be thinking about Grace and Donato at a time like this, not of his own needs. What sort of a friend was he anyway? He shook his head angrily. After all they'd gone through, all they'd suffered, everything had to be all right with these babies—*had to be*. Anything else was unthinkable.

Unbidden, a sweet little face topped by silky black curls formed on the screen of his mind. Paolo, Donato's first child, who had been so loved and so cherished, and whose death had caused such devastation. They had grieved for him and they still grieved, they always would, and although the twins wouldn't take his place they would help to soothe the ache he knew Grace and Donato still lived with.

He glanced at his watch, his eyes narrowing as he saw that some thirty minutes had elapsed since they had arrived at the hospital. Where the hell was Donato anyway? He'd give it another five minutes and then—

The door opening brought him swinging round to see Claire entering with a tray holding two cups of coffee. 'Donato's here. He's gone straight in,' she said shortly.

'And Grace?'

'She's OK. They think it will be an hour or two yet before she gives birth. She...she's in a lot of pain,' she added, so quietly he only just caught what she had said, 'but they appear to think that's normal.' She hadn't meant to say that last bit, it had just popped out of its own volition.

'Hey, come on.' He wasn't distant now. His voice was warm and husky as he moved swiftly to her side, taking the tray from her hands and placing it on the coffee-table before enfolding her into his arms. 'This is all new territory to me and you, but do not forget they have been through it before. Everything will be all right.'

'You don't know that.' Her stomach was churning violently, but to her chagrin she knew it was less out of worry for Grace—real though her anxiety was—and more because of the terrible enchantment of being held so close to the big male body she had dreamt about every night for weeks.

'This is a first-rate hospital and the facilities are second to none,' he said softly, resting his chin on the top of her head as he shaped her against his frame, moving in such a way that her hands crept round his waist as he snuggled her into him. 'Grace is young and healthy, and the babies are a good weight...you only have to have seen Grace over the last weeks to know that,' he added with wry amusement.

'But they're early—'

'Two, at the most three weeks,' he countered tenderly,

'which is nothing with twins—especially when the mother resembles an elephant!'

'Romano!' But she was laughing now, and as she relaxed against him, shutting her eyes for a moment and breathing in the heady fragrance of clean male skin and expensive aftershave, he felt his loins tighten and swell, and after a moment moved her from him to look down into her face.

'Is that coffee you brought in with you?' he asked lightly. 'Because I could certainly do with a cup.'

'Oh, of course.' He had retreated again, gently this time, kindly even, but just as implacably as before, she thought numbly, feeling the rebuff right down to her toes. And that hug—it had clearly meant as little to him as if he'd been hugging his grandmother. Whereas she... She had felt the contact in every nerve and sinew, and a few other places she could well have done without. It was humiliating, embarrassing to feel this way about a man who barely knew she existed. But at least he couldn't read her mind, he didn't know what she was feeling, and she'd rather die than let him guess.

For the first hour after they had drunk their coffee Romano was the suave, amusing companion he had been on one or two other occasions, exerting himself to keep her entertained and her mind off what was happening a few rooms away. And although she was aware it was a façade that he had perfected it was nevertheless engaging. As time went on, however, she noticed his eyes moved more and more often to the door until, some two hours and thirty minutes after they had entered the hospital, Donato made an appearance.

'Is everything all right?' They had both risen to their feet, but even as Claire asked the question she knew everything was *not* all right. The information was there to read in the set of Donato's face and the tightness of his mouth.

'They are talking about the possibility of a

Caesarean.' Donato's voice was calm; his eyes were anything but. 'The first baby, the one already in the birth canal, is not coming as it should, and Grace is getting tired.'

'Oh, Donato...'

'Please, do not worry, Claire.' Donato was quick to reassure her, but all three of them knew his heart wasn't in it. 'She is in the best place for any decisions that need to be made. Look, I must get back, but I just wanted to say that if you two want to go home...'

'No.' Romano's answer was instant. 'We will wait.' He turned to her as he added, 'You wish this?'

'Of course—you know I do,' she said quietly.

'Yes, I know.' His eyes held hers for a long moment and then he stepped forward, hugging Donato to him briefly before he pushed him gently towards the door. 'Go on—go back to her,' he said softly. 'Everything will be well.'

They sat in a stunned kind of silence for some minutes after Donato had left, the muted sounds of the hospital filtering through to their quiet little room now and again, and then Romano began to talk, his defences lowered by his overriding worry for his friends.

Claire knew she was in a unique position, that she was hearing things he had probably never expressed before, and she sat quietly at first, barely breathing.

'Nothing can be allowed to go wrong with this birth—*nothing*. Not after all they have gone through. When I think of all the children who are unwanted and unloved, born to parents who have no time for them... But Grace and Donato are not like that.' He was staring at her without really seeing her. 'They loved Paolo so much it was almost painful to see them all together. They will love these two in the same way.'

'I know.'

'You were born into a happy family?' he asked, his eyes focusing on her troubled face.

'Yes, very happy,' she said quietly. 'I have five older brothers, so I was teased unmercifully, but I always knew they would have done anything for me, and Mum and Dad loved us all. We had a lot of fun together, the eight of us.'

'*Sì*, this is how it should be.' He smiled mirthlessly, his eyes remote again as he looked inward. 'My mother gave birth to me just twelve months after she married my father, and fortunately I was the heir my father wanted. I say fortunately because if there had been girls before me they would have had to endure the same love-less existence I did, and I would not wish that on any child. My father's life was his own small empire. He lived to exert power and make money, nothing else mattered, and he was easily the most ruthless individual I have ever come across. I have seen him break a man, emotionally and mentally, and take great pleasure in doing so.'

'But your mother—she wasn't like that?' Claire asked softly, trying to hide the horror she was feeling.

'My mother was a social animal of the highest order,' he said quietly. 'She lived to entertain and be entertained. I heard her say on numerous occasions when I was growing up that if she had had to endure another pregnancy she would have killed herself, and there is no doubt that she meant every word.'

His beautiful dark eyes registered her shock and he smiled coldly, the black eyebrows twisting sardonically. 'You do not think a woman could feel like this? Oh, I assure you it is true,' he said softly. 'Not that she had a particularly bad time, as I understand, she just couldn't bear the physical changes of carrying a child. I do not think she ever forgave me for what she termed the most debasing and degrading experience of her life. So you see she too was unutterably thankful I was the required heir and her duty was done.'

'But...but when you were born they must have loved

you,' Claire protested weakly. 'Especially as they both wanted a boy.'

'I was given to a nanny on the day my mother returned from hospital, and as far as she was concerned that was that. My father would visit the nursery periodically throughout my childhood, to check on my progress and order the necessary retribution if I wasn't making sufficient headway, and my mother... I really do not remember her visiting my quarters once, although I suppose she must have done at some time or other. I was normally taken to her.'

He took in her anguished face and smiled, a real smile this time that melted the ice in his eyes. 'It is all right, Claire, it is not the tragedy,' he said softly. 'My nanny was a wonderful woman, and I think I was quite happy until she left to get married when I was almost seven. I was then sent away to boarding school, but in the holidays, when I came home, I saw Donato, and from the age of nine or so I spent most of my time at Casa Pontina when I was in Sorrento. The two sets of parents were friends socially, although I have often wondered what Liliana's private opinion of my mother was. Liliana was very maternal.'

Claire couldn't bear it. She just couldn't bear to think of him as a small boy, struggling to prove himself to parents who regarded him in much the same way as an expensive car—an appendage that reflected on them and must be seen to be of the very best at all times. He was acting as though it was all understandable, but what must it have done to his idea of himself, to his sense of self-worth? And she had thought he had had it all. Well, he had—all of everything that didn't matter a jot and nothing of anything that was really important to a child.

She forced the tears back with superhuman effort, knowing he would hate it if she cried for him, and managed to speak quite normally. 'So that is why you and

Donato are so close,' she said quietly. 'You must have been through a lot together.'

'He was, and is, the brother I never had,' Romano said simply. 'Through his mother I learnt what mother-love can be, his father always took the time to listen to me, talk to me, and Donato himself was a friend, a brother, who I knew would never let me down.'

'And then there was Bianca.' She had to speak the name, get it out in the open, although it was hot and caustic on her tongue.

'And then there was Bianca,' he agreed softly, the shutter she had seen so often before falling across his face.

'I suppose it was always expected you would marry her?' she asked painfully. 'With the two families being so close, and you growing up with her, it was the perfect outcome.'

'This was the general opinion when we announced our engagement.'

'I'm sorry you had such a short time with her as your wife.' Claire felt as though her heart were being torn out by the roots. 'It must have been devastating for everyone concerned—not just you, but Donato and Lorenzo—'

'You know she was adopted?' he asked suddenly. 'When it was not expected that Liliana could have more children after Donato?'

'Yes, I think Grace mentioned it once,' Claire said quietly.

'So there was no Vittoria blood in her veins,' he continued tightly, as thought she hadn't spoken. 'None.'

'I...' She didn't know what to say, staring at him with big brown eyes as she sought the reason for such a strange comment. Was he saying that in spite of looking on Donato as a brother, and on Liliana and her husband as substitute parents, the fact that Bianca had been adopted had made it easier to fall in love with her, that it removed the 'sister' connection? That must be it. She really couldn't think of any other reason for him stressing the point. 'She was very beautiful,' she managed at last, trying to keep her voice from shaking. 'I... You must have made a lovely couple.' It was pathetic, she thought numbly, but it was all she could think of through the whirling pain and jealousy and hurt.

'''A lovely couple...''' His voice was reflective, smooth, even, but possessed of such a coldness it made her shiver, and her eyes snapped up to his face again. '*Sì*, we made a lovely couple, Claire. Many people said this.'

Oh, she couldn't stand this, she just couldn't. It was destroying her.

'You know the old tombs, with their exquisitely carved effigies of marble and fine stone, often inlaid with gold and silver?' he remarked quietly, still in the same icy flat tone. 'People look at them and they marvel, do they not, at the craftsmanship, the beauty, the splendour of it all? But inside—inside is a different story. Inside there is decay and stench and dead men's bones.'

'I don't understand,' she said bewilderedly. Tombs? Effigies?

'No one could understand, Claire, unless they had been inside the tomb, seen for themselves the difference between the exterior and the interior, where the rot and the decomposition are exposed in all their grimness.' He leant forward slightly now, his eyes haunted as they looked into hers. 'But I have been there. I have seen.'

'Romano, what are you trying to say?' This was becoming surreal, misty. There was something she knew she should know, but was unable to grasp.

'Simply that—'

'*A boy and a girl!*' A tornado could not have made a more dramatic entrance into the room than Donato, his face beaming and his eyes alight. 'I have a son and a daughter—a son and daughter, Romano,' he shouted exuberantly, before his voice broke and he fell on his friend's chest with a cracked sob. 'I thought...I thought for a time back there—'

'I know what you thought.' Romano's voice was deep and husky, and as he hugged his friend his eyes met with Claire's over Donato's head and she saw they were wet.

'And Grace? She's all right?' Claire asked after a moment or two as Donato straightened.

'She is wonderful,' Donato said softly, with such a reverent note in his voice that it was all Claire could do not to smile. 'You must come and see the babies, both of you.'

'Now?' Claire stared at him in amazement. 'But should we? I mean, won't they mind?'

'They? They? Who are these "they"?' Donato bellowed ungrammatically, his face splitting in an ear-to-ear grin. 'No, "they" will not mind if our two dearest friends come to see their namesakes.'

'Their?...' Claire knew she resembled a goldfish, but she couldn't for the life of her shut her mouth.

'Little Claire Liliana and Romano Lorenzo.' Donato looked absurdly pleased with himself, before a look of horror came over his face and he clapped his hand to his mouth. 'Oh, I was not supposed to tell you yet,' he said quickly. 'It was to be a surprise.'

'It is.' Romano's voice was very dry. 'Are you sure about this, Donato? I would have thought one Romano in the family was enough?'

'We're sure.' Donato all but bounced towards the door. 'Come, Grace is waiting. She is very tired but she wants to see you both.'

The room in which Grace had been installed was of the sterile-clean hospital variety, but it was possessed of all the little luxuries that wealth made possible. Claire's eyes went straight to the two small cribs at the side of her friend's bed after she had hugged her close.

'Oh, Grace...' Two tiny black heads peeped out from

the blankets, one pink and one blue, and as she approached the see-through plastic cribs one of the babies, the boy, gave a huge yawn and little grimace before appearing to fall asleep again. 'They are beautiful—absolutely beautiful. I can't believe it,' Claire said softly, the tears running unheeded down her face.

'I know.' Grace bore a certain resemblance to a balloon that had been popped, and her next words added weight to the notion. 'The girl weighs seven pounds and the boy six pounds two ounces. Where did I put all that, Claire?' she said.

'And you didn't have to have a Caesarean, then?'

'No. The boy had got himself wedged, somehow, but he suddenly popped out like a cork from a bottle, even as the surgeon was preparing to scrub up, and the little girl followed within minutes.' Grace's voice was soft as she added, 'We'd like to name her after you, Claire, if that's all right, and the boy after Romano?'

'I told them,' Donato admitted shamefacedly.

'Oh, you're hopeless.' But the loving look she sent Donato said something quite different, and her voice was tender as she said, 'Give Claire to Romano, would you, Donato? And Romano to Claire?'

If only. As Claire's arms opened to receive the blue blanket, complete with baby, Grace's words echoed in her head like some sort of mocking refrain, and her eyes were blurred as she looked down into the minute little face encircled by soft wool. If only.

'She is so tiny.' There was a note in Romano's voice she had never heard before, and she lifted her head to glance at him, so big and dark and masculine, standing with the baby cradled tenderly in the curve of his arms. 'I cannot believe her little hands—so perfect,' he added in a shaky whisper, the look on his face as he gazed at the sleeping baby causing a huge lump in Claire's throat and a hot stinging in her eyes. 'And you will be loved, little one,' he said softly. 'You will be treasured all the days of your life.'

She saw Donato grip his friend's arm for a moment in silent understanding before he said, 'You will be their godfather, Romano, as you are Paolo's?' She knew Donato's present tense was not a mistake, that he and Grace were including their first child in this moment of celebration and that he was as real to them as the two children cradled in their arms.

'Of course. I would be honoured.' Romano didn't look up as he spoke, his gaze riveted on the baby's wrinkled little face.

'And you, Claire, you will be their godmother?' Grace asked quickly. 'Please say yes.'

'I wouldn't dream of saying no.' Her voice was tremulous, and as she looked down at little Romano Lorenzo again, the wonder of his tiny, perfect features and wispy black hair gripping her heart, she wondered if she would ever hold a child of her own in her arms. She didn't think so. She couldn't marry someone she didn't love, and how could any man follow Romano?

A tear dropped onto the baby's face, and she was just wondering how she was going to get through the next few minutes without breaking down completely when a stout and very austere-looking nurse bustled into the room, and then stood looking askance at them all.

'I think it is time we were leaving.' Romano smiled as he handed the baby in his arms to Donato and then turned to the nurse, saying something swiftly in quiet Italian which brought a smile to the nurse's somewhat grim face before she shooed them both out after Claire had placed little Romano carefully back in his crib.

'They are beautiful. I just can't believe how beautiful,' Claire said softly as they walked down the corridor in something of a stupor. Grace had hugged her tightly before she had left, and it meant more than any words could have done. 'What a miracle.'

'*Sì*, it is a miracle.' Romano felt as though every support had been knocked from under him. He would never have believed how the sight of the two tiny babies, products of Donato and Grace's unquestionable love, would have affected him, and to combat the growing feeling deep in the essence of his heart his voice was unnecessarily harsh as he said, 'Grace will be even more glad of your friendship now, for the rest of your short stay in Italy. When are you thinking of going back to England?'

The words in themselves could have been a flattering observation followed by a polite enquiry, but the tone of his voice was neither complimentary or friendly, and as Claire came to an abrupt halt Romano actually walked on a pace or two before he realised she had stopped.

'Claire?' He turned to meet her blank stare. 'Is something wrong?'

The emotional roller coaster that she had been experiencing ever since arriving in Italy, and which had been far more turbulent in the last few hours, shot the words out of her mouth without any conscious thought on her part. 'I think it should be me who is asking you that, don't you?' she said coldly.

'Meaning?' He raised superior eyebrows, his voice cool.

'Oh, don't give me that line, Romano. I'm not into playing games,' she bit back furiously, the pain and confusion of the last few weeks, added to the bitter-sweet poignancy of the time they had shared in the waiting room and then the moments with the babies, making this latest rebuff all the harder to take. 'You were rude just now—admit it.'

'I merely asked—'

'I *know* what you asked!'

'Then I do not see the need for these...dramatics.' His icy demeanour did not impress her in the least; she was far too enraged to be intimidated this time.

'Don't you? Don't you indeed?' she said grimly, moving close to him now and glaring up at him with furious eyes. 'Well, it may come as something of a surprise to you but when you talk to people as though they are less than the dust under your feet, it hurts. Amazing, I hear you say,' she continued, with deep and savage sarcasm, 'but true, nevertheless. You might be rich and powerful and handsome, Romano Bellini, but a little of the milk of human kindness is worth more than anything you've got.

'And another thing—' she stepped back a pace but without lowering her gaze, which was fixed tightly on his white face '—I shall leave Italy when I'm good and ready, and not before. And no comments from you one way or the other will alter my mind one iota. *Got it?*'

'I have, as you say, "got it"—crystal-clear.' Dark colour had flared across the classical cheekbones, but otherwise his face was as white as a sheet, his black eyes glittering with a rage that matched her own. 'I do not know what brought on this little tantrum, but I certainly get the message—along with half the hospital, I should imagine,' he added coldly.

'I really don't care,' she declared wildly, the pain and hurt and sheer unfairness of it all making her see red. 'I don't care what people think, Romano. I don't care that I sound like a fishwife, or that you are making this out to be all my fault, because *I* know it isn't. You were being nasty back there, after the babies and everything. How *could* you?'

'Claire—'

But she had stepped back another pace, and his outstretched hand met thin air as she turned on her heel and ran a few feet down the corridor and into the ladies' cloakroom they had just passed. She shot the bolt on the door with shaking hands before she slid down the hard wood and onto the floor, there to cry until there were no more tears left.

CHAPTER SEVEN

How could she have said all that? It was the thought that had been burning on her mind ever since the night the twins were born, but it was always much stronger when Romano was present and she could actually see his tall, commanding and very austere figure in front of her.

Even now, six weeks later, she still found it difficult to believe that she had actually yelled and screamed at him the way she had, that she had dared to. But he had made her so mad, so angry...

When she had emerged from the ladies' cloakroom a full twenty minutes after she had flown into it, her face washed and clean and her hair brushed into gleaming order, Romano had been waiting on the other side of the corridor, leaning with easy grace against the snow-white wall.

She hadn't known what to expect—recrimination, fury, contempt, outrage—but he had expressed none of these things, merely levering himself away from the wall as she shut the cloakroom door and indicating the corridor with a wave of his hand. 'Shall we?' he had asked levelly, his voice flat. 'I have telephoned Lorenzo and told him the good news so he can now go to bed. I thought it only fair.'

'Yes, of course.' She was surprised at how steady her voice was, considering how she was feeling inside, and the fact that the trembling that was churning her stomach couldn't be seen on the outside was something to be thankful for—especially as Romano resembled a block of stone.

They drove back to Casa Pontina without another word being spoken, and all the way she was deciding what to say when he dropped her off. She shouldn't have said all those things in the circumstances, with Grace and Donato and the babies and everything, it had been stupid—but she couldn't bring herself to apologise either. She wanted to, especially now the initial rage had gone and she was starting to think about all he had said about his childhood. Her heart twisted as though a knife were being plunged in repeatedly, but something inside, something that was raw with hurt and blinding pain, wouldn't let her.

And so, when he drew up outside the magnificent old house, she managed a stiff, 'Thank you—goodnight,' which he answered just as stiffly before slamming her door shut with a savagery that said far more than words could have done and striding back round the bonnet and into the car.

The engine started with a fierce growl and he swung the car round in a violent arc and sped off back down the drive in a blur of screaming metal, leaving her standing on the steps in the quiet of the night, pale and drained.

He rang her the next morning, very early, before the rest of the household, apart from the maids, were awake. Gina tapped on her door, her face apologetic as Claire struggled out of a deep sleep that hadn't come until the dawn had well and truly broken. 'It is Signor Bellini.' The maid had indicated the telephone extension by the side of the bed. 'He wishes to speak with you, *signorina.*'

'Hello?' Claire spoke gingerly as the maid left the room. 'This is Claire.' The fact that she wasn't really awake enabled her to sound both distant and calm.

'I apologise for calling you at this early hour but I think we cannot leave things as they are. Grace will be home with the children tomorrow and I do not wish her

to be upset in any way.' His voice was clipped and terse
and her antagonism was instant, banishing the remnants
of drowsiness and bringing her to immediate and furious
life. 'I would like us to go out to dinner tonight, to get
the air cleared, *si*?'

'I really don't think that's necessary, Romano,' she
said tightly, her fingers clenched so hard round the receiver that her knuckles gleamed white. 'I have absolutely no intention of upsetting Grace—so as long as you
don't there is no problem, is there?'

How dared he? How *dared* he suggest she was going
to run to Grace and pour out all that had happened when
Grace was so vulnerable? Couldn't he see she was made
of better stuff than that? And what about *her* anyway?
It obviously didn't matter at all that she had been upset.

'What happened last night was just between the two
of us. I am sure we can carry on as normal for the sake
of Grace and the children,' she added coldly, her heart
thudding.

'So you are refusing to have dinner with me?' he
asked grimly.

'Like I've said, it's not necessary. Grace and the
babies are my first concern—my only concern,' she said
firmly, the beat of her heart so loud now it was making
her feel sick. 'So you can rest assured there is no air to
clear. Good morning.'

She had put down the phone on the sound of him
speaking her name and promptly burst into tears—something she had continued to do fairly often over the last
six weeks when she was alone, she reflected now, trying
to ignore the sight of the two men playing football with
Lorenzo on the big lawn close to the pool.

She and Grace were sitting under the shade of the
spreading branches of a huge willow tree some distance
away, the two babies fast asleep in their carrycots between them with the odd grunt and snort to reassure
Grace that all was well.

Claire purposely turned in her seat now, so that her back was to the pool as she reached for Grace's hand and said, 'They are going to be fine, you know. You don't have to keep poking them to make sure they still squeak.'

'I know.' Grace grinned shamefacedly. 'I really do know. It's just that they are so perfect and I love them so much. Lorenzo is marvellous with them, isn't he? I think he's quite fascinated, actually.'

'So's Benito.' Claire shook her head gently as she went on, 'If I hadn't seen it with my own eyes I would never have thought a parrot could be in love, but he's as near to it with these two as anything else. He's gone all soppy.'

'He's more than just a bird,' Grace said, with a peculiar note in her voice. 'If it hadn't been for him—'

'What?' Claire leant forward as Grace stopped speaking. 'What were you going to say?'

'If it hadn't been for Benito I don't know if Donato and I would be back together again,' Grace said slowly. 'We'd got ourselves in such a muddle, such a tangled web, and he helped out, that's all. Donato laughs at me, but I know Benito can think and reason—he's more intelligent than some people I know.'

'And certainly more vocal.' Claire's voice was slightly astringent. The parrot had taken to linking her and Romano's names together at every opportunity, and although Grace and Donato laughed, assuring her it was because of the babies, she didn't think so. He had done it more than once before the babies were born, and always with that long drawn-out 'ummmmm' which sounded so terribly thoughtful. It was as though the bird knew the secret desires of her heart and it made her uncomfortable. As did the secret desires, she admitted wryly.

The last six weeks could be likened to a form of painful torture, she thought as she settled back in her seat.

After the furore of the night at the hospital she had expected that Romano would keep his visits to Casa Pontina to a bare minimum—enough to prevent Donato and Grace from suspecting all was not well but that was all. But instead it seemed as though he was forever popping in.

But that was probably what he always did, and May had been a beautiful month of clear blue skies and radiant heat that had just begged for barbecues and outside meals, she told herself wanly. It was natural he would choose to be with his friends rather than in the solitary splendour of his own home.

But it didn't help her deal with this love that had persisted in growing in spite of all her efforts to the contrary. She felt like a cat on a hot tin roof most of the time, forever aware of a tall, dark presence brooding in the background whatever she was doing. Like now. She turned and glanced over to where the men were now lazing by the pool, and even from some fifty yards away the somnolent power in the big, relaxed body made every muscle tighten.

Why couldn't he have a paunch? she thought crossly. Or bow legs? *Anything* to help combat this overwhelming attraction that was as physical as it was mental. And that was another thing—the more she had got to know him over the last few weeks, the more she had seen him with the family—especially Lorenzo, with whom he displayed a tender understanding that caught at her heart time and time again—the stronger her love grew. It wasn't fair. It just wasn't fair—but Grace still needed her here so she was trapped, like a pathetic little fly in the web of a big black spider.

She was aware of the very second the two men stood up, as Lorenzo leapt into the sparkling clear blue water of the pool, and of every step they took as they walked over the bowling-green-smooth lawn to where the women were sitting.

'The sun, it is burning hot.' Romano's eyes were hidden behind dark sunglasses as he spoke and she really wasn't sure if he was addressing her or not, but then he threw himself down by her feet and looked up at her, his jet-black hair, still a little damp from his swim in the pool some minutes earlier, curling slightly onto his tanned brow. 'You are wise to keep that fair English skin protected.'

'It isn't that fair,' she protested quickly, feeling, as she always did with him, that there was some slight intended. 'I'm not exactly a blue-eyed blonde, am I?'

'More of a velvet-eyed, smooth-skinned nervous little foal, I would say.' His voice was low and deep, but quite loud enough for the others to hear, its tone almost expressionless.

'I take exception to the "nervous".' She spoke lightly, the way she did to Lorenzo in one of their bantering sessions, but the analogy cut deep. He didn't have to remind her that she wasn't one of the voluptuous sensual females that seemed to be everywhere now the summer had started, she thought painfully. She was all too aware that the minuscule bikinis that covered the tiniest amounts of flesh on the slim golden bodies populating the beach were not for her—never again. And most of the girls were stunning, clothed or unclothed, anyway, with a confidence in themselves she had never had even before the accident.

'You are brave, then? Fierce, like the tigress?' he asked softly, the sunglasses hiding the expression in his eyes and his dark, hard face giving nothing away.

She hesitated, not sure if he was being nasty or merely teasing her a little. 'I don't know about fierce,' she said after a moment or two, 'but I'm not jumpy or neurotic, if that is what you were suggesting.'

'Not at all,' he murmured lazily. 'That would be most uncourteous, would it not?'

'Well, I don't suppose that would stop you for a min-

ute if that was what you were thinking,' she answered
frankly, before realising that she had let her tongue run
away with her again.

'Ouch, I had forgotten that even little foals can give
a hard kick if provoked.' But he was laughing, in that
unrestrained, husky way that made her pulse beat a little
faster and made her want to leap into his arms and cover
his face with kisses. All of which would not exactly be
appropriate, she thought as her heart gave one of the
strange little jerks it was wont to do in his presence.

'Come and have a swim.' He was looking at her again,
and she just knew that the conversation that had gone
before had turned the invitation into a challenge. 'The
water is beautifully warm.'

'Romano, the water is freezing,' Grace interrupted
laughingly. 'I had a swim earlier and it's really cold.'

'You see—everyone has had a swim except for you,
little foal.' He reached up a lazy hand and removed the
sunglasses, his eyes narrowed against the splashes of
bright white light filtering through the branches overhead. 'Donato and Grace are able to look after their children for two minutes while you cool down.'

The 'cool down' was a dig, indicating that he had got
under her skin, she thought balefully as she looked into
the handsome face staring up at her. Which he had. But
there was no way she was going to admit it.

'Of course they are,' she agreed lightly. 'But I'm not
dressed for swimming.' She indicated her sleeveless sun-
top and long cotton skirt. 'Besides which we need to eat
before long; I'm starving. Shall I go and ask Gina and
Anna to bring out the food?' she asked Grace, standing
up as she spoke.

'I'll come with you. There are a couple of bottles of
Rubino di Piave in the cellar that will go very well with
steak and chicken,' Grace said easily. 'We'll sort them
out while the men get the barbecue going. OK, Donato?'

'No problem.'

No problem? Oh, she wished there wasn't a problem, Claire thought desperately as she walked back to the house with Grace, the sun burning hot on her unclad head and the air sweet and soft and richly scented. But there was—a huge, gigantic, gargantuan one—and these cosy foursomes, or sevensomes if you counted Lorenzo and the babies, she added wryly, were testing her to the limit.

Everything was against Romano ever feeling anything for her; in her brain she knew that. He was hugely rich, a sharp-witted and cynical man of the world who, in addition to his power and good looks, was possessed of a certain something that drew women to him like a magnet. He could have any woman he liked and he must know that. He would be viewed as the ultimate catch for most of the unattached women he came into contact with. And as if all that wasn't enough he had been married for some years to a stunningly beautiful woman he had clearly adored and still wasn't over. And she—she was not beautiful, stunningly or even mildly.

Why had he wanted her that night? Her brow wrinkled as she sought an answer to the question that had plagued her for weeks, and the only reply her heart gave her was…availability. She had been available, there at hand. It hurt, it cut deep, but she couldn't lie to herself. Everything he had said and done had made it clear it would have been a one-night stand, something pleasant but meaningless…to him. And to her? It would have destroyed her. She just couldn't have given herself to him and then walked away as he had expected. She couldn't.

He had seen her as a pleasant diversion and she had seen him—saw him—as the man she would love for the rest of her life. There was no meeting point.

The barbecue and the afternoon passed like the ones before it, pleasantly, with lots of lively conversation and tongue-in-cheek banter—to all intents and purposes an enjoyable Saturday spent in the company of good friends. But later that evening, as the adults sat drinking coffee in the drawing room with the windows open to the last of the dusky light, Claire knew if she stayed one more minute in the room she was going to shout and scream and tear her hair out.

'It's getting late.' She stood up slowly, as though her head wasn't near to bursting point, and gestured to the gardens outside. 'I think Lorenzo is still down by the pool. I'll fetch him, shall I?'

'Gina or Anna will do it,' Grace said quickly.

'No, it's all right, I'd rather. I've got the beginnings of a headache and a few minutes in the fresh air might clear it.' Claire gave the bright, sweeping smile she had perfected in the last few weeks, which brushed over Romano's face in just the same way as it did the others. 'You all finish your coffee. I won't be a minute.'

Once outside she stood for a moment with her eyes closed and her face lifted to the darkening sky, oblivious to the river of grey and gold above her and the faint twitterings and melodious birdsong all around as nature settled down for the night. The air was still beautifully warm, but without the fierce heat of the day, and a faint breeze touched her face in a whisper of a caress.

Grace or no Grace, she would have to leave here— and soon. She had a solid ache in the place where her heart was all the time now, and everything about Sorrento was getting deeper and deeper into the very fibre of her being, its influence insidious.

Grace was coping wonderfully well with the babies and she had plenty of help with Anna and Gina to hand. She knew her friend had appreciated her presence before the birth of the twins and in the early days afterwards, when she had been a little tearful and emotional, but she was back to being the old Grace now—happy and perfectly content.

She began to walk down to the pool as her thoughts solidified. Yes, she would go soon—maybe even next week. She was beginning to feel so lacerated inside she really couldn't stay any longer.

'Help! Please...' For a moment, a split second after she heard the cry and gurgling moan she froze, and then she was running over the grass like the wind, calling as she went.

'Lorenzo? Lorenzo, I'm coming. Hang on—*hang on*...'

How long Lorenzo had been struggling in the water she didn't know, but she could see immediately that he had cramp, his face and body contorted in agony and his mad thrashing frightening as he went under the water.

She leapt straight in, surfacing just a few feet from where he had gone under. She could see he was still moving under the water and that he wasn't on the bottom of the pool, and she dived down beside him, grasping him round the chest with one arm as she made for the life-giving air above them.

They surfaced once, both gasping and spluttering, but Lorenzo's panic-stricken struggles and her long skirt, which had draped itself round her legs, made keeping afloat impossible, and they went under the water again in a mad tangle of limbs as Lorenzo pulled her down with him.

Without thinking about it, she kicked away from his hold, her hands tearing at the fastening of her skirt. Once she was free from its constriction she grasped Lorenzo again, his back against her chest as she forced them both up through the water that was suddenly such an enemy to the surface.

'Relax—relax. Listen to me, you'll drown us both...' She doubted if Lorenzo could hear her as he gasped and choked and twisted in her hold until he was facing her, his arms locked round her neck in a stranglehold, and then they were going down for the third time—and she began to feel as frightened as he was.

The relief she felt as Lorenzo's arms were whipped from her neck made her limp for a moment, but then, as she felt herself being hauled upwards by her hair, the pain made her kick out for the light above.

'Claire? You are OK for a moment?' She was aware that she was sucking in great mouthfuls of air, her eyes and nose and throat smarting and burning, but she managed to nod and gasp, 'I'm all right—go on,' as Romano let go of her and concentrated fully on Lorenzo, who was horribly still.

By the time Romano reached the side of the pool Donato and Grace were there to help haul Lorenzo out, and as Donato turned his younger brother over and began to apply artificial respiration, which almost immediately caused Lorenzo to choke and heave, Romano cut through the water again to Claire's side.

She was still trying to breathe. 'It's all right, I'm all right...' she gasped. But he took no notice of her protestations, turning her round and drawing her back to the side of the pool with his arm round her chest.

'Claire—oh, Claire.' Grace was almost hysterical. 'We didn't hear you. Donato and me, we didn't hear you, but then all of a sudden Romano was up and out of his chair like a bullet. Oh, you could have drowned— you could have both drowned.' She was kneeling by the side of Donato and Lorenzo, the latter now sitting up in his brother's arms. 'For this to happen...'

'Enough, Grace.' Romano's voice was soft. 'She is quite safe. But perhaps you can go ahead and organise baths and hot drinks for both of them and we will follow. Donato, you will take Lorenzo?'

Donato was clearly in shock, it showed in the whiteness of his face and the way he was clasping Lorenzo to him, but he nodded slowly, rising with Lorenzo in his arms as Romano helped Claire from the pool.

And it was only in that moment, when it was far too late, that she realised the worst had happened. Her concern for Lorenzo, her own fear and shock and the numbing effects of the water, had blinded her to the fact that her skirt was gone and her brief, bikini-style pants revealed most of her stomach.

She knew he must have seen the faint, thread-like lines that were pale and silvery on her skin, even though the hard, handsome face remained the same in the second before he lifted her up into his arms, but there was absolutely nothing she could do about it, she realised with sickening clarity.

'I can walk. There's no need—'

'Be still. You are not walking. You almost drowned out there,' he said tightly. 'Why the hell didn't you call me?'

She could feel his hair-roughened chest against her cold skin as he held her close to his heart, his shirt having come open in the rescue, and the touch and feel and texture of his maleness was causing her head to swim. Nevertheless, she rallied sufficiently to say, with some heat, 'Don't be so stupid—there wasn't time. I heard him call and I knew I had to get there at once.'

'At risk to your own life?' he bit out grimly. 'If I hadn't heard you call the pair of you could be lying at the bottom of the pool by now, do you realise that?'

'It's not my fault.' She couldn't believe they were having this conversation, and the unfairness of it brought hot tears to the back of her eyes. 'Are you saying I should have let him drown? I couldn't... There just wasn't time...'

'Shh...shh.' As her voice wobbled he stopped and lowered his head, looking down at her with glittering black eyes, his face all planes and shadows in the dusky scented gloom. 'I really do not know whether to spank you or kiss you, do you know that?' he said surprisingly.

It was so unlike anything she had expected him to say

that she could only stare at him with great liquid eyes, her body continuing to register the thrill of his taut maleness, the slight muskiness of his skin, the raw sensuality in his face.

'Claire...' His voice was husky and low, and he paused for a moment before he continued, 'You were brave—very brave.'

He had been going to say something else, she knew it, and she also knew it would have come from the heart of him, the real man, which was why the drawbridge had suddenly been raised so swiftly. Something had stopped him. She remembered his eyes on her skin, and felt a disappointment and pain so acute it stopped her breath.

Damaged goods. The accusation was there, hot and sharp, before she fiercely denied it—and him. 'Let me down. I can walk—'

'You are not walking,' he interrupted tightly.

'You can't tell me what to do—'

'Well, it is about time someone did.' And then his mouth had claimed hers, possessing it hungrily and with something approaching fury. His breathing was ragged as he crushed her into him, their wet clothing accentuating the hard thrust of her nipples against his muscled chest and the damp heat of their bodies as desire rose.

Donato had disappeared by now, and in the last few minutes the shadows of night had encroached quickly, the sky a charcoal blanket overhead with the first stars already beginning to make their appearance. The birds were silent, and there was no sound to be heard from the house in the distance or from the world beyond Casa Pontina's boundaries. They could have been the only two people alive.

She was beginning to tremble in his arms, he could feel it as she was aware of the furious pounding of his heart, and as he slowly lowered her against him, so her feet were on the ground and she was held into the length of him, his hands began to touch her, stroke her, caressing the soft, smooth skin of her back under the light top.

She shivered as his warm lips moved over her neck, her throat, her ears, unable to stop him, to say and do all the things she knew it would be sensible to do and say. This was love, then, she thought helplessly, this longing to be one with him body and soul, to be utterly enveloped in him to the point of oblivion, to know that his needs were more important than hers, that she would do anything, anything for him.

She didn't know how her hands had come to be tangled in the strong, virile black hair, but as she pulled his mouth back to hers he groaned softly, exciting her senses and causing her to move against him in such a way that they both became bathed in sensation.

She brought her hands from his shoulders, where her fingertips had been digging into his skin in her excitement, and tentatively slid them inside his shirt, touching the hair-roughened muscled skin of his chest with delicate, exploring fingers. She had wanted to touch him like this for so long and now, as she felt the passionate heat of his skin and the arousal of his hard nipples in their lair of black silk, she couldn't believe what it was doing to the core of her.

He was kissing her mouth again, biting gently at her lower lip and letting his tongue-tip stroke against the contours of the full upper one before he penetrated the sweetness within, his thrust greedy. 'I want you. I'm burning up inside. You do not know what you do to me, little foal...'

His murmur was hot and desperate against her closed eyelids, his voice thick with desire, and everything in her rose to meet the need he was revealing. She wanted him. She wanted him so fiercely that her blood was pulsing and racing with it. She wanted to hold him, touch him, taste him, feel him inside her, draw him into the very kernel of her being.

The strong, predatory thrust of his arousal against her soft, silky flesh told her he was as helpless in this tide of passion that had taken them by storm as she was, and she knew she had to draw back, to stop, but she couldn't remember why. Every thought she had ever had was burnt up in this one moment, and then the next, and the next... There was no past, no future. Nothing existed outside the immediate present in all its erotic intimacy.

His hands were moving all over her, everywhere but the smooth, soft curve of her belly, and then his fingers splayed across that too, and she knew their tips would sense and feel the slight breaks in the silkiness. Instinctively she reached down and drew them to her waist as a tiny thread of sanity returned. This was madness, madness...

Even as the warning brushed her mind Donato called from the darkness, his tone anxious. 'Romano? Romano, you are coming to the house?' The intrusion into the bubble that had captured her senses was complete, and she jerked away violently, her face flaming as she took two steps backwards, away from him.

'Claire?' He reached out and pulled her against him before she could resist, holding her firmly but not making love to her now as he said, 'I did not plan for that to happen. You have to believe me.'

'Do I?' She stared up at him, her inner turmoil reflected in her eyes. How could he touch her like that, show such warmth, such passion, without it meaning something to him? But it didn't. Now that the spell was broken cold, harsh reality had taken its place. 'How did it happen, then?'

'You have to understand—' As Donato's voice interrupted them again he swore once before calling back, 'In a moment—we will be there in a moment,' without taking his eyes off her stricken face. 'Claire, you have to understand that I can't give you what you want—'

'Which is?' she cut in shakily.

'Commitment—any sort of real commitment.' The words hung there for a second, stark and chilling, before he said, 'That is what you want in a relationship, *si*? I know that. That is why I haven't touched you in the last weeks—' He broke off abruptly, shaking her slightly before he said, 'Don't look at me like that. This may not be what you want to hear right now, but it is the truth.'

'Then why tonight?' she asked with painful directness, her heart pounding.

'I do not know why tonight,' he said, with a flatness to his voice that made her blood run cold. 'I did not mean it to happen, but you were so— Oh, hell, you almost drowned,' he added, with a savagery at variance with what had gone before.

'So you were being kind, trying to be nice to me?' she asked in a small, quiet voice. That was it—he felt sorry for her. He had seen the scars, sensed her embarrassment, and he was trying to be nice to her. She wanted to die.

'Kind?' He stared at her as though she were mad. 'What has kindness to do with anything?'

'You…you felt sorry for me,' she stated flatly. Her voice was as expressionless as his had been previously, but her whole body was beginning to shake with a reaction to all it had been through since she had first heard Lorenzo call.

'Do not talk such rubbish, woman—' he began tightly, only to stop abruptly as he took in her trembling. 'Dammit, you're cold. You will be ill. I should never have kept you out here.'

He had whisked her off her feet again before she realised what was happening, but she felt too weak and spent to make any protest, shutting her eyes and keeping them shut even when Romano carried her into the house and up the stairs to her room. It was only after he had placed her carefully in the big cane chair in her bathroom, and Gina and Anna were fussing around her, that she forced herself to enter the land of the living—and only then because she knew he had gone.

'Lorenzo?' she asked faintly, cutting into the maids' effusive praises as they stripped off her top and panties and helped her into a steaming bath.

'He is OK—he is very OK, *sì*?' Gina said reassuringly, running still more hot water into the bubbly scented foam. 'The *signore* and *signora*, they are with him, and he just have the...how you say?...the sore throat, *sì*? From the water he swallow? But he OK. The doctor, he come soon.'

The doctor did come soon, and after he had finished giving Lorenzo the all-clear he came along to Claire's room, popping his head round her door to observe her lying pale and wan against the heaped pillows, her hair spread out in a shining chestnut arc behind her as she allowed the last traces of dampness to dry in the warm room.

Grace had been in and out for the last little while, flitting between Claire and Lorenzo's rooms like an anxious mother hen. But now the twins had woken and were demanding their dinner so she was occupied in the nursery—for which Claire was thankful. She wanted nothing more than to shut her eyes and go to sleep, to blot out the thoughts that were screaming and shouting in her head, painful, torturous thoughts.

'*Ciao*, Claire.'

She liked this doctor. He was the same one who had attended Grace before the twins' birth and she understood he had been the Vittoria family doctor for years. 'Hello, Doctor.' She tried to smile, but to her horror in the next moment she had burst into tears, and he was sitting on the bed patting her hand like a comforting old woman.

It was a minute or two before she could control herself, but he said nothing, quietly waiting until she had

dried her eyes and then saying slowly, 'Is this just because of the swimming incident, or is there something
more, Claire?'

'I...' She blinked into the wise old face for some moments, and then decided honesty, or partial honesty at
least, was the best policy. 'There is something else, a
problem that has been getting me down,' she said
slowly. 'I...I feel it would be better if I left Italy, that I
could cope better at home, but I don't like to walk out
on Grace when she needs me.'

'I think it was good that you came when you did, and
I am sure you would be welcome to stay for as long as
you like, but the crisis has passed, *sì*? Grace can manage
perfectly well now, I am sure.' He smiled at her and she
managed a tremulous smile in return, her brown eyes
swimming. 'This...problem—it is an affair of the heart?'
he asked perceptively, and when she nodded, went on,
'*Sì*, it normally is at your age.'

'You think Grace doesn't need me here any longer?'
she pressed again. 'Really?'

'I think she likes having you here, but, no, I do not
think she needs you in the way you mean,' he said quietly. 'Grace is an intelligent woman. She knows you
have your own life to lead and that this time was tem-
porary. I am going to give you something to help you
sleep now, and in the morning you can review the situation and do what you think best with a clear head. Now
is not the time for decisions of this nature.'

She lay very still waiting for the pills to work once
the doctor had left, her eyes moving slowly round the
beautiful room and her mind picturing the rest of the
house and the gardens beyond. She would miss Casa
Pontina, she would miss Grace and Donato, and Lorenzo
and the babies, but, oh, she had to leave—she *must*. This
evening, that time in the garden when Romano had held
her in his arms, and now this talk with the doctor—all
told her that her time here was finished.

She didn't need to wait and review the situation and her head had never been clearer. She loved a man who was as far out of her reach as the man in the moon. A man who could have any woman he wanted to satisfy his physical needs, a man who was powerful, wealthy and handsome. But worse, much worse, she loved a man who was in love with someone else—albeit that the object of his devotion had been dead for three years.

Since that evening in the hospital, when he had told her about his parents and his loveless childhood—the way he had relied on Donato and his family for everything that should have come naturally from his own kin—since then she had known deep in her heart that there was no chance, ever, for her. Because Bianca had been his childhood sweetheart and more, much more than that. She had been part of the good side of his life, from when he was a boy, a necessary and integral part of himself. She could see that now.

He might have had other girlfriends, played around a bit the way wealthy young bachelors in his privileged position were almost expected to do, but Bianca had known she'd had his heart, and when the time was right he had seen it too and married her. The perfect couple. Until fate, in the guise of a fast sports car, had taken a hand, that was.

Her eyes were dry now—achingly, bitterly dry. The pain was too deep for tears.

CHAPTER EIGHT

'A FAREWELL party?' Romano's eyes shot from the invitation in his hand, which Grace had just handed him, to Claire's face. 'You are leaving?' he asked tightly. 'When?'

'In a couple of weeks.' She was amazed her voice was so steady. This was the first time she had seen him since the pool incident three days earlier, although he had telephoned the house the morning after to enquire as to how she and Lorenzo were. 'And Grace is insisting on a party.'

'Of course I am. You've made loads of friends since you've been here and they'll all want to say goodbye. Poor Attilio is heartbroken,' Grace added, still in the same conversational tone of voice, as she glanced casually at Romano. 'Claire's told him she's too busy for romance, but I think the poor lamb thought while she remained in Italy there might be a chance for him. I think they'd make a lovely couple actually, don't you, Romano? And he blames himself now for taking his month's holiday these last four weeks, but it was all arranged before Christmas; he was touring France with some friends.'

'Was he?' Claire had never heard Romano use such a cold and uninterested tone with Grace before, but her friend didn't appear to notice.

'All that time lost—he's quite distraught.' Grace laughed lightly. 'Still, he's got two weeks left to get her to change her mind,' she added, with another glance at Romano's glowering face.

What on earth was she talking about? Claire thought

138

bemusedly as she stared at Grace. Her friend knew she wasn't interested in Attilio in the slightest, and it wasn't like Grace to discuss anything of this nature so frivolously—especially as she knew the tutor's infatuation with her made her both uncomfortable and embarrassed.

'Anyway, I must go and speak to Cecilia about dinner. Are you staying, Romano?' Grace asked over her shoulder as she made for the door. 'You know you are welcome.'

'No, I am sorry, I have a previous engagement,' he said flatly. 'I just came to see—to see how you all were.'

A previous engagement? Claire thought painfully. She didn't need to be the Brain of Britain to work out the gender of his dinner companion, not with him in full evening dress and looking dark and dangerous.

'Have a drink anyway—and fix Claire one, would you? I'll be back in a moment,' Grace said sunnily as she shut the drawing room door, leaving them alone.

'You would like a drink?' he asked her coldly, his eyes narrowed as they moved over the brilliant sheen of her hair and creamy skin to the soft, dusky red of her mouth, where they lingered for an infinitesimal moment.

'No, not really—would you?' she asked nervously.

'No, I do not want a drink, Claire.' She hadn't seen him in this mood before and she couldn't quite determine it; the dark eyes were glittering with some emotion that was undefinable. 'So, you are breaking poor Attilio's heart and returning to England.' It was a statement, not a question. 'I did not expect you to leave Grace with the infants so soon.'

It was said coolly and without the slightest expression but was unmistakably a criticism, and immediately her hackles rose. 'Didn't you?' She managed a disdainful smile that was the best bit of acting she was ever likely to produce. 'You don't think Grace is an able mother?'

'Of course she is,' he said at once, his tone one of shocked outrage.

'Well, then...'

'But I thought you had come as a friend, a companion,' he said silkily. 'Someone to talk to and share with. This is a very emotional time for a woman—'

'I don't need you to tell me that,' she bit out tightly, enraged beyond measure that he dared to preach to her about emotional times. Him! Of all people! After what he'd put her through. 'But Grace had her low time before the babies were born—some women do—and she's fine now. And I've...I've got things to see to in England.'

'What things?' The words were rapier-sharp but she was determined not to be intimidated. He saw her as some sort of pathetic spinster who had nothing better to do than dance attendance on one of his friends, did he? Grace was Donato's wife, and as such, in his opinion, one of the privileged few who were entitled to any consideration? Well, she'd got news for him...

'Things of a personal nature,' she said dismissively.

'That is no answer,' he grated out harshly.

'Well, it's the only one you're getting.' He didn't want her, not for anything beyond a brief fling at least, and she wasn't even sure about that any more.

She had replayed the incident in the garden over and over in her mind, and however she tried to skirt round it, to make it different, the fact that he had been trying to reassure her about her femininity because he had felt sorry for her was uppermost. And perversely she both loved and hated him for it—loved him for the understanding and tenderness it revealed, which she had sensed before was a hidden part of his nature, and hated him because the last thing, the very, very last thing in the whole world that she wanted him to feel for her was pity.

'I see.' He eyed her grimly.

He looked very arrogant and very handsome as he stood frowning at her, the tall, broad-shouldered body that was so unequivocally male shown to perfection in its clothing of somewhat traditional evening garb, emphasising so well the hidden strength and power of the hard frame.

Of all the men in all the world she'd had to go and fall for this one, she thought painfully, with more than a touch of self-despair. Her mother had always said she didn't do things by halves, and she had been proved right once again.

'Will you come to the party?' she asked carefully, after a few tense moments in a screaming silence he didn't seem inclined to break.

'Do you want me to?'

'Of course,' she said flatly. 'Donato and Grace would be upset if you refused.'

'Donato and Grace. Yes, I see.' He stared down at her with narrowed dark eyes. 'In that case I shall be there.'

'Good.' For Donato and Grace. Oh, she hated him...

'And now I really must be off. It would not do to be late,' he said, with that cool control that hid all expression.

'No, you mustn't keep her waiting.' She didn't know why she had said it. The only good thing was that her voice sounded bright, carefree, even, and not at all as though she was eaten up inside with jealousy and a longing to know who he was meeting and what she looked like.

'Quite.'

Game, set and match to him, Claire thought numbly as he smiled with that icy twist of his lips that didn't reach his eyes, before inclining his head and leaving the room. Well, he could see who he liked after all. He was a free agent—no strings, none of his hated commitments. She swore, once but with great intensity, in her mind, and was so shocked at the profanity that she hurried out of the room to find Grace or Lorenzo—anyone to stop her mind from following such a self-destructive path. She was going to get through this with mind and soul intact; she *was*. She wasn't too sure about her heart, but she would have to gather the pieces of that and deal with it once she was back in England.

The almost daily visits Romano had been making for the last few weeks became a thing of the past, and Claire didn't see him again until the day of the party.

It was the middle of June and the day was a hot one, the temperature creeping steadily upwards towards ninety degrees Fahrenheit. The careful sunbathing Claire had indulged in over the last few weeks had turned her clear skin a soft honey-gold, and the coppery tint in her silky chestnut hair was more pronounced, flattering the darkness of her eyes and making them appear enormous.

She and Grace had made several shopping trips into Sorrento over the last two weeks, the winding streets and fascinating alleyways providing everything from the very best fashionable clothes and exquisite jewellery to simple handicrafts and cheap souvenirs.

After an hour or two of serious shopping they had whiled away any remaining time before Grace had had to get back to feed the twins at sunny pavement cafés, where they had sipped coffee and nibbled at wickedly rich cream cakes whilst watching the world go by.

It should have been an idyllic interlude before her return to England, and Claire had worked hard to make it so for Grace, but all the time, whatever she was doing and whoever she was with, the tall, lean figure of a dark Italian intruded onto the screen of her mind.

Still, she thought now, as she glanced again at the beautiful cocktail dress in ivory brocade hanging in her wardrobe, at least she had found the perfect dress for the party. She had balked at the price at first—it had seemed outrageously expensive for a strapless, above-the-knee bit of nothing—but once she had tried it on she was hooked. The dress had fitted like a glove—tight, but not too tight—and the cut and design flattered her figure like nothing she had worn before.

'Oh, it's perfect, Claire, you've got to have it.' Grace had tried to buy it for her but she had insisted on paying for the dress herself, and she had known exactly why she was buying it. He wanted nothing to do with her—fine. He felt sorry for her—not so fine. But tonight she was going to go out of his life with a bang, not a whimper, or die in the attempt!

But all that would come later. For now she was going to go down to the pool with Grace and the children for the afternoon and *relax*—something she was finding harder and harder to do these days.

She turned from the wardrobe and walked over to the huge mirror by the window, there to gaze at the bikini-clad figure that stared back at her. She had bought the bikini on the same day she had bought the dress, and she recognised it was something of a statement—although she hadn't actually analysed what it was saying.

Her fingers moved slowly over the faint marks on her stomach as she mused into the big brown eyes looking back at her. This was her—good or bad, perfect or imperfect. It was *her*, and she wasn't going to hide from herself again. All over the world people coped with far, far worse, and they did it with integrity and courage too. Well, she might have lost her way for a time, concentrated too much on what had been spoilt rather than what she still had, but she wasn't going to do so again.

She was fortunate, very fortunate, and she was going to count her blessings every day, every hour, every minute, for as long as it took for this dense black cloud that enveloped her from morning to night to lift.

And what if it never lifted? the probing little voice in the back of her brainbox asked softly. Then she would cope with that too. She would have to.

The rich scent of summer was heavy on the warm, slumbering air as she walked down to the pool where

Grace and the others were already in residence. Donato, Lorenzo and Attilio were in the cool, spotlessly clean water, thrashing about in a mad game of tag which seemed almost violent.

She was glad to see Lorenzo entering in with such gusto. The boy had been a little nervous for a few days after his close escape from drowning, but he was now as confident as ever, if a good deal wiser.

They had discovered that he had sidled into the kitchen and coaxed a huge supper out of Cecilia just minutes before the near fatal swim, and also that he hadn't bothered to keep up his fluid intake during a day of energetic exercise in the hot sun—something that Donato had warned him about time and time again.

A ten-minute lecture in Donato's study had ensured that neither mistake was likely to be repeated again.

In spite of the noise from the pool she must have fallen asleep on the big cushioned lounger under the shade of the trees, because when some sixth sense made her open her eyes it was to see Romano lying next to her, clad only in a pair of breath-stoppingly brief swimming trunks, his dark eyes narrowed on her face.

'*Ciao*, Claire,' he said softly, his tanned, muscled body turned fully towards her as he lay on his side, one arm supporting his raised head.

If she'd been fully *compos mentis* the sight of that near naked, perfectly honed male body just a foot or so away would have knocked her for six; after surfacing from a deep sleep she found the effect devastating, and she was frozen to the spot.

'Grace has taken the infants in to feed them and Donato and Lorenzo are helping to set up a marquee on the big lawn for your party. Grace thought it would be good to eat outside tonight,' he continued quietly. 'All is bustle and excitement.'

'Except here.' She sat up as she spoke, painfully aware that he had watched her as she slept, had been able to inspect every inch of her body as she had lain vulnerable and still. She didn't like that. She suddenly found that it was one thing to make brave new principles and wear her bikini for the rest of the world, and quite another to do so if Romano was around.

'Except here,' he agreed softly.

'Shouldn't...shouldn't you be helping Donato?' she said quickly. 'And I really must go and see if Grace—'

'I wanted to talk to you.'

'Oh.' It stopped her garbled panic as though cutting through it with a knife. 'Why?' she asked warily.

'I just wanted to know what your plans were, that is all,' he said calmly, 'and whether you intend to return to Italy in the near future—I know that Grace would like this.'

The brief ray of hope died, although her heart still continued to thud against her ribcage so hard it was painful. 'I would like it too, but I don't think it's possible,' she said quietly, drawing on all the strength she possessed not to break down in front of him. She drew her knees up to her chest, dropping her chin on them and letting the silky veil of her hair hide her face as she said, 'The last two months, being with the twins and helping Grace change them and look after them, has made up my mind about something, and I feel I ought to do it now before all the doubts and uncertainties get in the way again.'

She heard him swing his legs off the lounger but she didn't look at him, even when he spoke again. 'May I ask what that thing is?'

'I am going to work with children again,' she said slowly. 'The accident I told you about, when Jeff left me, well, it was a bad one—a very bad one—although it wasn't my fault. But the other driver died; he was only eighteen. I had the children I was nannying in the car with me, and...and I lost my nerve for a time—a long time. I was frightened of being responsible for anyone again, I suppose.'

'They didn't...?'

'Oh, no, they weren't badly injured,' she said hastily. 'In fact it was only minor cuts and bruises and concussion, and they were allowed home the next day, but...but it could have been different and that's what kept haunting me—that and the crash itself. I...I was in hospital for some time—abdominal injuries and broken limbs but thankfully no permanent damage—but...but the scars on my stomach were nothing to the ones in my mind,' she finished painfully.

'Claire—'

'But I love children and I love working with them and I've made up my mind I won't let the past beat me,' she said quickly, before he could continue. She didn't want to hear words of comfort, not now; she wouldn't be able to take it.

'You are very brave.' There was a note in his voice that made her draw her head up in spite of herself, and when she looked at him she saw his face was very white, with a small muscle working in his jaw, and his body was stiff and still. 'Very brave.'

'No, not really,' she said sadly. 'Not most of the time.' Not over you. I will never be brave over you... The knowledge that soon she would never see him again was suddenly overwhelming with him there, in front of her, and something of the dread and horror that had pierced her heart must have shown on her face because he suddenly reached out to her, moving swiftly as he shifted over to her lounger.

'The worst is over. You have faced your demons and conquered them,' he said urgently as he took her into his arms, turning her round so she was half sitting on his lap. 'But why not give yourself more time—work here with the twins while you get used to the idea? Grace would love that—'

'No, I can't—'

As he took her mouth it fused with his own in a kiss that was all desperation and fire. The pale honey-gold of her body was almost translucent against the satin darkness of his skin, the jet-black body hair that covered his chest and limbs making his skin look even darker and hers paler in contrast.

They clung together for long minutes as he crushed her fiercely against him, his mouth exploring hers in an agony of desire. 'Stay—you know you want to stay,' he said at last as he lifted his head to look into her dazed face with glittering eyes. 'I only have to touch you and a fire consumes us both. You know this is true.'

'Yes, I know,' she murmured helplessly.

'Then stay,' he said imperiously. 'Stay in Italy.'

'I can't.' Everything in her wanted to agree to his demand, to melt against him, to take anything he was prepared to give for as long as he was prepared to give it. 'You know I can't.'

'I know you are fighting the fire, Claire, and you cannot win,' he murmured huskily. 'It would be good between us, you must know this. You cannot tell me that your other boyfriends, this Jeff, even, made you feel like this? When I take you it will be as though you are the first—I am the first. The earth will explode and there will only be us. You must know this, *feel* it?'

'Don't, Romano...'

But her protest was lost as he kissed her hungrily, his hands and mouth arousing her to fever-pitch until tiny little moans sounded deep in her throat.

'You see?' He raised his head to look down into her flushed face. 'You see what you would be denying us both? This is nothing, *nothing* to how it could be when the two of us are alone and the whole night is before us. I want to touch you, kiss you, taste every inch of your body, take you into that timeless world where there is only sensation and pleasure.'

He wanted her. He *wanted* her. And this wasn't pity, she told herself tremblingly. However Jeff had viewed the marks on her body they didn't matter to Romano, she knew that now, but...

'But you don't love me.' Her mouth expressed her thoughts and she arched away to look up fully into his dark face. 'And one day you would leave me.'

'Love is an illusion, Claire, apart from for the favoured few,' he said urgently. 'What we would have is far more substantial, more real—a fusing of our bodies—'

'Love is not an illusion, Romano.'

She knew, in the split second before she said it, that this would be the end, but she couldn't endure much more of this without agreeing to everything he said, and then she would be lost, mindless, a puppet to be picked up and dropped at his will, or when his sexual hunger needed sating. So she needed to finish it—now—and she knew only the truth would do that.

'I know because I love you,' she said woodenly, a tiny part of her wondering at the fact that in all her wildest dreams she had never imagined telling him that in order that he would leave her.

He remained perfectly still for what seemed like an eternity, and then shook his head slowly, his eyes fixed on hers. 'No, you do not. You are mistaking physical desire for something else—something that is propagated by novelists, the film world and the media for their own ends, something that does not exist for the vast majority of us.'

'I would like to believe that, Romano.' She moved away from him, sliding down the lounger and then standing to look down at him as her heart cracked open and slowly began to bleed. 'It would be wonderful to believe that, the way I feel right now, but I know it isn't true. Don't ask me how I know that I love you, that I'll keep on loving you, because I can't really give you an answer. It's just something here, deep inside, that is as real to me as taking the next breath.'

'You thought you loved Jeff.' He rose now, standing so the length of the lounger was between them, and his voice was harsh and cold. 'You were going to marry the guy, for goodness' sake.'

'I told you about that—he wasn't honest with me and I was fooled by him; it was that simple.' This was killing her, *killing* her. 'But this isn't like that. Perhaps I had to taste the counterfeit to know the real thing, I don't know, but you've been honest—blatantly honest,' she added painfully, 'and I'm under no illusion that you can return my love. However, the way I feel makes it impossible for me to stay in Italy. I'm sorry, Romano, it just does.'

'You are running away—'

'No.' She stopped him with an upraised hand, her chin rising and her back straightening. 'No, I am not running away. I am leaving. That is quite different. I didn't mean to lay all this on you. I wouldn't have, except...'

'I pushed you into it,' he ground out grimly.

'Perhaps it's for the best—I don't know.' She shook her head, her silky hair stroking her face from which all colour had fled. 'But I do know I can't stay. If I go now it ends cleanly, with some dignity, but if I stayed...if I stayed I'd turn into the sort of woman I despise—a little toy, a marionette, just waiting for the next phone call, the next time you wanted me in your bed.'

'It would not be like that.' He raked his hair back from his forehead in a gesture of sheer frustration. 'We would be friends, companions too. It would not just be sex—'

'*I can't be your friend, Romano.*' Her voice was too shrill and she lowered it quickly, clasping her fingers into tight fists at her sides as she prayed for control until this was finished. 'Don't you see? I want more, much more than that, and in the end I'd be like a millstone round your neck. You'd grow to hate me and I might even grow to hate you too, even as I loved you. I want it all, you see.' She couldn't stop the tears falling but she spoke on through the pain and anguish, knowing she had to make him *see*. 'I want all of you—everything. To be your friend, lover, wife, the mother of your children, the companion you're with in old age—all of it.'

He looked stricken now, his face as white as hers with a tinge of grey that spoke of his own inner turmoil.

'And I know that can't be, that your heart is buried with Bianca, that you wanted all that with her and she was taken from you…'

She couldn't say any more, her voice trailing away in a muffled sob as she turned and ran, ran as though her life depended on it, along the length of the pool and out into the garden towards Casa Pontina.

And even then—foolish, stupid, ridiculous though it was—a tiny part of her hoped he would follow her, catch her before she reached the house, tell her he had realised now, at last, that there was some hope for them, that he could perhaps learn to love her.

But he didn't. And she reached the house and her room. And then there was just silence.

CHAPTER NINE

'CLAIRE? Claire, are you all right?'

At the sound of Grace's voice outside her door Claire turned from the window where she had been standing in numb silence for nearly an hour, too devastated even for the relief of tears.

She had done and said everything she'd promised herself she never would—why, *why* hadn't she kept quiet? she asked herself with genuine horror. But it was too late now to count the cost; the deed was already done and her humiliation was absolute. And yet, in the exact same circumstances, would she do any different if she had the time over again? She turned the thought over in her mind as she walked across the room to the door. No, not really. It had seemed, no, it *had been* the only way to make him understand that she had to leave and not return.

Oh, Romano... She leant her forehead against the wood for a moment before she opened the door. She would have suffered humiliation a thousand times worse if only it could have made him love her.

'Claire?' Grace was standing on the landing, her vivid blue eyes shadowed with concern. 'Is anything wrong? I don't mean to pry but Donato said you ran back to the house as though the devil himself was after you, and that Romano left without saying goodbye. You...you haven't argued or something, have you?'

'Not exactly.' Claire gazed at her wearily. 'But something *is* wrong—terribly wrong—for me at least. You'd better come in for a minute and I'll tell you.'

'I don't want to pry—'

'No, I want to tell you,' Claire said quickly. 'It's only right that you know, Romano being Donato's best friend and all. Perhaps I should have told you before, but I didn't want to worry you or spoil things. Anyway, I'm going now, and you should know. The bare facts are that I've fallen in love with Romano and he doesn't feel the same. He's just attracted to me—physically, that is.'

'Oh, Claire.' Grace sat down on the bed with a little thud. 'Does he know? That you love him, I mean?'

'That was the cause of me running back to the house and him disappearing this afternoon,' Claire said grimly. 'He'd got in mind that we could have some fun together, a light affair—something very grown-up that would end amicably with no hard feelings and where we could still be friends—but I couldn't see it that way.'

'I should think not.' Grace glared into the distance. 'Men! They're on a different planet from us, aren't they?'

'Admittedly he didn't know I loved him then.' Claire sighed. 'I should think now he does know he's congratulating himself on a lucky escape. He looked…he looked quite horrified.'

'Did he say he didn't love you?' Grace asked carefully.

Claire nodded dismally. 'He doesn't believe in love, real love, any more. I think that when Bianca died his feelings went into cold storage. Perhaps he'll never meet anyone else he can care for the way he did her.' It was agonising but she had to face it.

'*Bianca?*' Grace's eyes shot to her face. 'He said he still loved her?' she asked incredulously.

'More or less.' Claire walked across to the window again, looking down into the gardens below with her back to the room. 'Anyway, regardless of all that, he doesn't love *me*, and I can't stay feeling as I do. You understand that, don't you?'

'Of course I do, but…' Grace's voice trailed away and

she made a small sound of exasperation in her throat. 'Oh, Claire, there's so much I want to tell you but I don't feel it's my story to tell. I made a promise—' She stopped abruptly and then said, 'Bianca wasn't what she appeared, that's all I can say, and I've really thought over the last few weeks that Romano was interested in you.'

'Interested?' Claire laughed bitterly. 'I think he'd tell you that himself, but only as far as how we'd be in bed together and that's not enough for me—not feeling as I do. Look—' she turned round to face the room, forcing a smile to her face '—don't look so tragic—it's not the end of the world. I'll get over it.' *Never*, her mind shouted.

'For now we've both got to get ready for the party, and then I'll only have another day with you. We aren't going to spoil it talking about this. Go on, go and start getting ready and I'll do the same,' she said brightly, walking across and giving Grace a hug before ushering her to the door. 'We'll eat, drink and be merry, yes?' Her words mocked her.

'I feel awful about this, and I can't believe Romano has behaved so badly,' Grace said miserably as she stepped onto the landing. 'I feel I don't know him.'

'He hasn't, oh, Grace, he hasn't,' Claire said quickly. 'He told me right from the beginning, when he realised we were physically attracted to each other, that a short affair was all he could offer. He was totally up-front, it was me that...well, you know. The trouble is I didn't choose to fall in love with him,' she added quietly, her brown eyes liquid pools. 'It just happened. I didn't want it to.'

'I know.' Grace stared at her for a moment and then hugged her again before turning and walking quickly away, her head bent.

This was going to be one riot of a party, Claire thought grimly as she forced herself to turn on the shower and begin preparing for the night ahead. Grace would tell Donato and that would mean both of them would be feeling uncomfortable and upset, and the very last thing in the world she felt like doing herself was smiling and chatting and being sociable. Romano wouldn't come, of course...

She stripped off the bikini and stepped under the warm silky water in the smart shower cubicle, letting the flow wash over her upturned face for some minutes before she began to wash the chlorine out of her hair. But she couldn't have fobbed Grace off with an excuse, not again, not after what Donato had seen and surmised. What a mess. What an incredible, tangled, painful, *messy* mess.

'You look *gorgeous*.'

As Claire walked into the drawing room where Grace and Donato were sitting waiting for the first guests to arrive her friend's undisguised admiration and Donato's open-mouthed stare confirmed what the mirror had already told her: the dress had been worth every penny. The only trouble was the person it had been bought for would never see it.

Nevertheless, their reaction enabled her to say, with a lightness that was purely manufactured but which she hoped would put them at their ease, 'Do I normally look that bad, then?'

'Not at all.' Donato recovered first, leaping to his feet and smiling as he said, 'What would you like to drink? Your usual white wine?'

'No, not tonight.' Tonight she needed something more than white wine to get her through. 'Is that one of your cocktails you're drinking?' she asked brightly, indicating the glass of pale amber liquid Donato had placed by the side of his chair. The golden frothy drink looked as harmless as ginger ale, but to the uninitiated it had the kick of a mule, and that was just what she needed, she told herself desperately. 'I'll have one of those, if I may.'

'What a good idea.' Grace, who never touched anything stronger than wine herself, nodded in agreement. 'I'll have one too.'

'Right.' Donato clearly didn't consider it a good idea, but just as clearly he wasn't going to argue in view of the circumstances.

By the time the first guests arrived some thirty minutes—and two cocktails—later, Claire was feeling a little more relaxed and Grace was positively fluid—so much so that Donato removed his wife's glass with its last dregs and carefully refilled it with fruit juice.

'Well, here we go, then,' Grace muttered in an aside to Claire as they heard Anna open the door and speak a welcome in volatile Italian. 'The party from hell is about to begin.'

'Oh, Grace.' She hadn't thought anything could bring a smile to her lips tonight, but her friend's dramatic comment, which nevertheless exactly summed up how she was thinking about the evening, managed it. It somehow confirmed Grace's love and support too, more than any flowery words or demonstrative shows of affection could have.

The party did begin, and continued to move on, but that was the most Claire could say about it. She smiled until her face ached, laughed and chatted and accepted the numerous compliments that came her way with grace and aplomb, avoided Attilio's love-lorn gaze whenever she could and smiled brightly at him when she couldn't, and all the time her heart was breaking.

There seemed to be so many subtle reminders of Romano within the elegant, wealthy crowd. The elusive whiff of aftershave on clean male skin, the way the odd male held his head, an occasional husky laugh, the broad set of a pair of muscled shoulders...

'How are you doing?' Grace slipped a supportive arm around Claire's waist as she murmured in her ear, 'Donato is full of admiration for you and the way you're handling this, you know.'

'Is he?' It was no comfort at all.

'I'm going to announce the food is ready in the marquee in a minute, and there'll be dancing on the main lawn afterwards—the band's just arrived. You will eat something, won't you?'

'Of course I will. Stop worrying,' Claire said quietly.

She did manage to force a small amount of the food Attilio insisted on fetching past the lump in her throat, but her plate was still three-quarters full when she pushed it away. Dusk was beginning to cast blue-grey shadows over the garden, and already the hundreds of tiny lights that were threaded through the surrounding trees twinkled and shone in the dim light.

The whole scene—the exquisitely dressed women with their elegant partners, the beautiful garden with the majestic lines of Casa Pontina in the background, the lilting music from the band to which several couples were already dancing—took on a slightly unreal quality as she gazed around, becoming dreamlike, illusory.

'Claire?' Attilio rose from his seat beside her, bending slightly as he stretched out his hand. 'You will dance with me? Please? I would like to have that to remember,' he added, somewhat pathetically.

'I don't really feel like dancing, Attilio.' The thought of any other man holding her in his arms was obnoxious right at that moment, besides which the band were playing a slow, romantic number, and she didn't want to encourage the desperate devotion that had been on Attilio's face all night into something else.

'Please?' He continued to stand there, his hand outstretched, and after a few embarrassing moments when she was aware of covert glances in their direction, she rose to her feet.

'Just one dance, then,' she said gently.

'Sì.' He smiled, a warm, adoring smile, and she wondered, for the umpteenth time that night, why she couldn't have fallen in love with the handsome young tutor instead of Romano. Everything would have been so simple then—so straightforward, so easy.

On reaching the dance floor he took her immediately into his arms, fitting her close against him as they began to dance—and he danced very well, she realised ruefully. He probably did everything very well, but he wasn't Romano.

'Claire, you will come back soon, *si*?' he asked softly, after a few moments. 'Here to Casa Pontina?'

It was the same question he had asked her a hundred times in the last two weeks and she gave the same reply as she always did, 'No, I don't think so.'

'But, Claire...'

And then she saw him, a flash of white catching her eye as she looked over Attilio's shoulder. Romano, resplendent in a white dinner jacket and dark trousers, was leaning lazily against the trunk of an old magnolia tree at the perimeter of the lawn, his lean body relaxed and still as he stared her way. The dim light, and the distance, made it impossible for her to see his expression but she knew, without the shadow of a doubt, that the black eyes were cold and condemning as he watched her dance with the other man.

She faltered, missing her step, and suddenly realised that she hadn't heard a word Attilio had been saying for the last minute. 'I'm sorry?' With a great effort she dragged her eyes away from the figure across the lawn. 'I was dreaming—what did you say?' she asked dazedly.

'I said—' He broke off as her eyes flickered from him again and half turned, following the direction she had been looking. 'That is Romano over there?' he asked quietly as he took in the remote, stationary figure in the distance.

'Yes—yes, I think so.' She had frozen at first, but now found a rising anger was beginning to take hold of her

senses. How could he? How *could* he act with such in-
sensitivity? she asked herself bitterly. What had he come
here for? A civilised goodbye? A neat tidying of the
messy ends? Well, he was in for a shock because she
didn't think she was capable of either tonight, right or
wrong as that might be.

She loved him. She had laid her heart bare before him
and told him exactly how she felt. Didn't he realise how
painful this was?

'Ah, I see. Now much that has puzzled me becomes
clear,' Attilio said thoughtfully, his eyes sad as they left
Romano and came back to rest on her face. 'This is the
reason that you leave Italy so abruptly, Claire?'

She thought about evading the question, even about
downright lying, but somehow she couldn't, and so she
nodded slowly. 'Yes.' She looked straight into Attilio's
eyes now. 'Yes, it is.'

He nodded in turn. 'So we both have the broken
hearts? I am sorry, Claire, I would not wish that it was
so. It would be a convenient thing if love could be turned
on and off—like the tap, you know? But it is not possible, is it.'

'No.' His understanding and sympathy was too much
in her vulnerable state, and as the tears flooded into her
eyes he pulled her close, his voice soft. 'I am sorry, I
did not want to make you cry,' he said quietly into the
shining silk of her hair.

'I know.' Her voice was muffled as she spoke into his
chest. 'It's just that I'm so sorry I've made you unhappy.
I didn't want to,' she added chokingly. 'Really, Attilio.'

'You do not have to tell me that. You are one of the
most gentle, kind—'

'I hate to interrupt this somewhat public embrace, but
I need to speak with you, Claire.' If ice particles had
formed in the air around them she wouldn't have been
surprised, so cold was Romano's voice.

Her head sprang up at the same time as Attilio's arms

tightened still further round her, and when she looked
into Romano's dark face at the side of them she saw his
eyes were blazing with an emotion that was hot and
caustic, his mouth set in a straight, grim line.

'Perhaps Claire does not wish to speak with you.' For
a moment she couldn't believe Attilio had dared to take
such a stance with Romano, and it was clear that
Romano was taken aback—but only for a moment.

His eyes narrowed into thin, glittering slits that threat-
ened to annihilate the slightly smaller man on the spot,
and as he took a step forward Claire jerked herself free
from Attilio's hold, her face flushed and distressed. 'It's
all right. I'll come.'

'Claire, you do not have to speak to him—'

The hell she does not,' Romano growled darkly.

'It's all right, Attilio, really.' She tried to dredge up a
reassuring smile but it was beyond her. 'I...I need to
talk to him. I'll be back soon. Please, people are looking.'

As the three of them left the group of people dancing
Romano took her elbow in a firm grip, only to swing
round violently as Attilio said from just behind them,
'You had better not hurt her—'

'It will not be Claire who feels my fist—'

'Romano.' She hung onto his arm and cast an ago-
nised glance of appeal at Attilio. 'Please, Attilio, just
leave it—please.'

As Attilio nodded and turned away Romano swore
softly and savagely under his breath, and then she was
being whisked across the garden by the bruising hand
under her elbow so fast she was sure she was going to
fall. She couldn't believe the ferociousness with which
the two men had confronted each other. To her knowledge they had never before had a cross word, and yet
for a minute back there it had looked as though they
were going to kill each other.

'You think I am a fool, is that it?' His words were a

low snarl as they reached a clump of sweet-smelling bushes and entered a different part of the garden, hidden from view for the party revellers. 'Embracing in full view of everyone with that...that clown?'

'We weren't embracing.' She jerked herself free so suddenly that he let her go, and then she turned to face him like a small tigress and spat, 'And what's it to do with you, anyway? Attilio is a friend—'

'I know what Attilio is,' he shot back violently, 'and also what he would like to be to you. Moreover, you know it too—full well. Given half a chance—'

'He didn't *get* half a chance.' How could you love someone so much that it tore you apart inside at the same time as wanting to leap on them and bite and scratch and destroy? she asked herself dazedly.

'No?' It was said with magnificent scorn. 'You could have fooled me.'

'Why should I want to do that?' she asked bitterly. 'Why are we even having this conversation? All that could be said was said earlier. I mean nothing to you beyond a romp between the sheets—a quick lay.' It was crude and it was blunt and it was *exactly* what was sending her half-mad with pain and regret, but she knew the second the words left her lips that she had gone too far.

She wanted to turn and run at the look on his face as he towered over her, his eyes glittering with unholy fire, but she was frozen to the spot, utterly terrified. She could hear the sounds of the party in the distance, feel the soft warmth of the Italian night on her skin, smell the sweet perfume of summer all around, but here, in this private little spot, she was completely at his mercy—and she had never been so scared in her life.

'This is what you believe?' he asked tautly. 'This is why you were allowing that moron to hold you, kiss you? And what would have come next if I had not made an appearance?' A hard hand fastened on her wrist as her wits returned and she took a step backwards, ready for flight. 'Answer me, Claire, what would have come next?' he bit out grimly, his grip tightening to steel on her soft flesh as he pulled her close to him again. 'A walk in the garden among the shadows of night? An intimate little interlude when he told you how much he loved you, that he could not live without you, that he must have you?'

'And what if he did?' she bit out furiously, her fright swallowed in the red-hot rage that was pulsing through her body in ever-increasing ferocity. 'I'm a free agent, aren't I? Just like you, Romano. No strings, no commitments, a little fun here and a light affair there—'

'You are not like that!' The words were torn out of him and he shook her none too gently, his eyes blazing. 'Dammit, Claire...' She tried to turn her head as she realised his intention but his lips captured hers before she could escape him, and in spite of everything—his arrogance, his accusations, the sheer unreasonableness of it all—she felt herself melt into him as her love for him took over.

It was crazy, madness. She was behaving like those women she had always secretly despised even whilst pitying them—women who allowed themselves to be treated as doormats, who became walking zombies controlled by the partners they adored... The thoughts were there, in the raging tumult of her head, but they carried no weight. He was holding her, kissing her, and that was all that mattered.

Maybe, if he had been rough, threatening, using his superior male strength to dominate and subdue, she might have been able to fight the weakness that had invaded her limbs. *Maybe.* But he was none of those things. He was cradling her against the broad, hard expanse of his chest, his mouth passionately tender and his strong hands moving over her body in an agony of desire as he tasted the sweetness of her mouth. 'Claire,

Claire…' His voice was a desperate murmur against her lips. 'I want you. I want you so badly…'

And she wanted him, more than he would ever know, she thought helplessly. Would it be so bad to take one night, one magical night of love that would have to last her for the rest of her life? She drove herself deeper into the hard frame of him, her response firing the desire that was shaking his body still more as his hand twisted the rich silk of her hair, bringing her head back and allowing him greater access to her mouth, her throat, the soft swell of her breasts.

She was quivering in his arms, he could almost taste her moistness, and the white-hot fire that was ravaging his body with a desire that was indescribable had taken him beyond the brink of holding back. This was what he had feared when he came here tonight. It had to stop—he had to stop. But he had never known anything like this before… The thoughts were tearing through his brain even as he lowered her onto the soft warm grass, the cool, hard control that he had prided himself on all his life consumed by heat.

'Claire?'

Grace's voice, made sharp by worry, cut through the night like a whistling blade, and had much the same effect on the two people hearing it.

'Claire? Where are you? Are you all right?'

Romano rose instantly, lifting Claire to her feet almost without her being aware of it, and then steadying her as she stood swaying, her eyes enormous and dazed and her hair tousled.

'We are here, Grace.' His voice was cold and contained, his handsome face dark and imperious with no hint of the passion that had consumed it moments earlier, and the shock of the transformation brought Claire to her senses like a douche of cold water would have done. She pulled herself from his hold, smoothing her hair with shaking hands and adjusting her clothing moments before Grace rounded the corner, stopping abruptly at the sight of them standing stiff and stony-faced in front of her.

'Are...are you all right?' Grace asked uncertainly as she glanced at Claire. 'I...Attilio said you had gone to talk to Romano and that you had been some time. He thought there might be something wrong.'

'But as you can see he was mistaken,' Romano said, with a silkiness that told Claire the other man's interference was something he would not forget. 'Claire is quite safe.'

'Oh, I didn't think...' Grace's voice trailed away for a moment before she drew herself up a little straighter and said, her voice resolute and determined, 'Do you want to come back to the party, Claire?'

Sisterhood. Romano's eyes narrowed slightly as he watched Grace move close to Claire and put an arm round her waist. He had heard of the phenomenon, of course, but the bright social butterflies and hard businesswomen he usually came into contact with didn't consider that sort of thing important. It was the final irony that of all the women he had known the only two that he could fully respect, one of whom he loved like a sister and the other, the other... He closed his mind to the searing groan at the heart of him. Both were now united against him. *Dammit...*

'Romano?' There was a faint thread of hope in Claire's voice, and something else—something that twisted his guts into knots. 'Do you want to...to say anything else?'

They stared at each other for a long, long moment, the tall, ruthlessly handsome and dangerously powerful man, and the slight, fair-skinned English girl.

Yes—yes, he wanted to say more, much more. He wanted to explain how it really was, appeal to that soft, voluptuous warmth that was at the heart of her, wrap himself in it, submerge all the torment and agony and just let it enfold him like a comforting blanket.

He wanted to possess her—*hell*, did he want to possess her... He was still as hard as a rock at the thought of what might have been if Grace hadn't interrupted them. He wanted to drive deep into that soft female body, fill it, stretch it until there was no room in her mind for anything but him. He wanted to take her to the brink of fulfilment and spend time touching and tasting her until they tipped over into the abyss of sensual pleasure that was pure undiluted sensation, and then he wanted to do it all over again.

He wanted to see her face as he possessed her so completely that he became her world, to feel every tiny movement, each rhythmic undulation that he knew he could bring forth from that warm, secret place deep inside the core of her.

He wanted... He wanted *her*—mind, soul and body— and the desire for the first two left him with no option but to walk away. He had known he shouldn't come here tonight; it had been an act of inexcusable self-indulgence, a need to justify himself, to explain the unexplainable. He couldn't take her into the hell he inhabited—

'Romano?'

The bewildered, tentative whisper was the final straw, and he stared at her one last time, his eyes taking in every contour of her face, the vulnerability in the liquid brown eyes, the tremulous quiver that her mouth was trying so hard to hide, and his own straightened into a thin, grim line.

'Goodbye, Claire.'

She didn't say anything, just continued to stare at him in silence as Grace hugged her closer, and then he turned, striding past her without glancing her way again.

CHAPTER TEN

'I'M COMING with you to the airport,' Grace insisted for the third time that morning, 'and I don't want to hear another word about it. The twins will be perfectly all right with Anna and Gina for a few hours, and it won't do them any harm to have the odd bottle now and again rather than me. You know that. Lorenzo will keep his eye on them too—you know how he is—and Donato thought he'd be home early this afternoon. So you see they'll have a whole host of admirers to dance attendance.'

'Are you sure?' Claire asked quietly. This would be the first time that Grace had left Romano and Claire since they had been born. At first Grace had been the original fussy mother, forever checking the infants when they slept and jumping at every little squeak and snuffle, but as the babies had grown and put on weight she had started to relax a little, becoming more confident both in the alarms fitted to the cots and also her children's health.

'Quite sure.' Grace smiled at her, knowing what she was thinking. 'I'm convinced at last they're here to stay, and part of that is due to you and all your straight talking and common sense. I...I couldn't have shared my fears with anyone other than you and Donato, Claire. I knew I had to work them through for myself but I needed to express them too.'

'I know,' Claire said softly.

'I just wish...'

'What?'

'That you hadn't got hurt in the process,' Grace said

slowly. 'He's an idiot, Claire, a first-class idiot. I don't know whether to hit him or pity him for what he's missing.'

Grace had said much the same yesterday, alternating between trying to find excuses for Romano's behaviour and bursts of righteous anger against her husband's best friend, and although Claire knew her friend meant well neither tack had helped the long, hot Sunday to pass any easier.

But now it was Monday morning, and her flight left Naples airport just after lunch. She had already said her goodbyes to Donato that morning, before he had left for his offices, and a somewhat tearful farewell to Lorenzo before he started his lessons with Attilio. She had kept her parting with the tutor brief and brisk, for his sake rather than hers, but nevertheless had breathed a long sigh of relief when it was over.

'Antonio has put your cases in the back of my car, so whenever you want to go I'm ready,' Grace said now, as they finished their third cup of coffee, having taken a long, leisurely breakfast that had continued long after the other members of the household had gone their separate ways.

'Right. I just want to say goodbye to Benito first— he'd never forgive me if I went without seeing him,' Claire said, perfectly seriously, and Grace nodded back, just as serious.

'Absolutely. He knows you're going, you know. He's been a real misery the last day or so.'

Benito was sitting on his perch on the patio of Lorenzo's sitting room, eyeing the door morosely as she walked through, his head tilted glumly and his exotic plumage shining in the clear white light of the sunny morning.

'Hello, old thing.' Claire walked across to him and stroked the silky feathers as she murmured softly, 'I don't want to go, you know, but I've no option. You do see that, don't you?'

'Benito—nice old bird,' the parrot intoned mournfully. 'Claire *e* Romano. Romano *e* Claire, eh?'

Did he really know? she asked herself silently. It seemed impossible and yet those bright round eyes were terribly understanding. 'I wish it was Romano and Claire, Benito,' she said softly. 'I really do. But I'm afraid you've got it wrong this time.'

'Wrong...wrong...' The melancholy tone was too much, and Claire felt a slight smile touch her mouth despite her misery. He was a comical old bird, she thought fondly, and she would miss him. She would miss everyone.

She looked past the parrot now to the gardens beyond, already shimmering in the heat of the June morning. The sky was a vivid sapphire-blue, devoid of the tiniest cloud, and the air was redolent with the smell of the crisply cut lawns that the gardeners had just finished working on. All was colour and warmth and light, the antithesis of what she was feeling inside.

'Ready?'

She hadn't heard Grace come up behind her but now she forced a bright smile as she turned away from both the view and her thoughts. 'Yes, quite ready.' She stroked Benito one last time and then followed Grace out of the room.

The airport was the same as airports everywhere—noisy, busy and possessed of a life of its own that went on regardless of the hundred and one little human tragedies being played out in the comings and goings within its ramparts.

Since leaving Casa Pontina, and during the drive into Naples, Claire felt as though she had gone into a vacuum, and that feeling continued as she checked in her luggage and was told the flight was slightly delayed.

'Grace, you go now—really.' She could tell that in spite of all Grace's brave protestations her friend was itching to get back to her offspring. 'You know how these delays drag on sometimes and I'm going to be quite happy sitting here. I've got a good book. I shan't be able to relax if I know I'm keeping you from leaving.'

'You're not,' Grace said stubbornly.

'Grace, I mean it—' She was going to say more but the sudden glassy look in her friend's eyes brought her head turning round. Romano was standing a few feet away, dark and still and magnificent in a black silk shirt that was unbuttoned at the neck and black jeans that hugged the lean, lithe body in a way that interfered with her breathing.

'Romano!' Grace recovered first, her usually warm soft voice sharp with outrage. 'What on earth are you doing here?'

'I would have thought that was perfectly obvious.' He smiled, but it was a warning, as the tone of his voice had been. 'I want to say goodbye to Claire.'

'You want...' Shock and disbelief were added to the outrage. 'I don't believe this.'

'There is something unusual in one person wishing to say goodbye to another?' Romano asked, with a mildness that was suspect, and then as Grace went to speak again he raised his hand, his face cold. 'Grace, I know you are Claire's friend, and I appreciate that, really, but she is quite grown-up, in case you had not noticed, and this is something that concerns only the two of us.'

He hadn't come to ask her to stay. Claire stared at the tall, dark figure and her heart thudded so hard it was painful. She didn't know how she knew, but she did, so the only other reason he would be here was to say goodbye, as he had indicated to Grace. Why was he putting her through this? She wanted to close her eyes and pretend it wasn't happening. It was unfair, cruel.

'Something that concerns only the two of you?' Grace

said, with a stiffness that spoke volumes. 'I'm sorry, Romano, but I don't see it that way.'

'Then that is your misfortune, not mine. But whether you approve or not I am going to speak to Claire, and alone.'

This was getting out of hand. She turned to Grace now, putting her hand on her friend's arm as she drew her gaze. 'It's all right, Grace, really. I'll...I'll talk to him. I'm OK, don't worry.'

'Of course you're OK,' Grace said encouragingly, in a tone that reeked of concern and doubt. 'Do...do you want me to go?'

'I think it's best. I'll ring you as soon as I get home,' Claire said quietly. 'The babies are waiting for you, and you don't want to be away from them too long.'

'OK.'

They hugged for a long moment and Grace's eyes were damp when she turned to go. 'Don't you dare, *dare* upset her again,' she said in a fierce undertone to Romano, which brought the thick black eyebrows winging upwards, but she was gone before he could speak, hurrying away with her head bent and her shoulders hunched.

'I think Grace has got carried away with this maternal thing.' His voice was low and deep, and she swung round from watching Grace disappear with hot words of defence, only to surprise a curious expression of vulnerability on the hard, masculine face. He was nervous, she realised with a little shock of surprise—uneasy, out of his depth. It was so amazing that she allowed him to take her arm and lead her over to a quiet corner away from the busy hubbub without protest, sinking down onto the seat as her legs gave way.

'Can I get you a coffee?' Now he had her alone he seemed strangely unwilling to get the goodbyes over, and she shook her head slowly, knowing her control was only paper-thin. She wanted this over—quickly. She didn't want to make a fool of herself in front of him again. She was past the burning humiliation she had felt for days after telling him she loved him and being rejected so thoroughly—her misery was too deep and intense for pride—but she didn't want his last memory of her to be of her crying and wailing and holding onto his shirt-ends, which was exactly what she felt like doing right now.

'No. Perhaps…perhaps you should just say what you came to say and then go,' she said quietly, the whiteness of her face belying her outward composure.

'Claire—' He stopped abruptly, and then sat down on the seat next to hers, taking her hands in his, his face desperate. 'I should not be here—or perhaps I should. I do not know any more. All I do know is that I could not let you leave Italy, and my life, without telling you the truth. I do not know if it will make it easier or harder—I'm past knowing anything right now—but…I have to explain.'

'What?' The look on his face was frightening her.

'You think that I loved Bianca, that I still love her, sì?' he said heavily. 'You think we had the perfect marriage, that it was—how do you English say?—the bed of roses, yes?'

'Yes.' She was feeling almost numb now, the way people felt when they had been injured so badly that their nerve-ends were cauterised with shock.

'Claire, my marriage was your worst nightmare come to life. It was days and weeks and months of unending torment and pain,' he said bitterly. 'There were times when I thought I was going mad, when I looked at the rest of the world and wondered how they could get it so right and I could get it so wrong.'

'Romano?' She stared at him, unable to take it in. 'I don't understand.'

'I have never understood it.' He shook his head savagely before taking a long, hard pull of air and letting go of her hands, turning in his seat and looking down at the floor, one hand clasping the fist of the other until the knuckles shone white. 'But perhaps I had better start at the beginning. I have told you how my childhood was, how Donato's family became mine? Donato and I, we were a little wild, headstrong, the way youth is, and we...how you say?...played the field, had fun.'

He was talking in a dull monotone now that was more chilling than the bitterness of before. 'Bianca, she was the little sister, *sì*? Donato's little sister. She meant nothing more. But when she reached fifteen, sixteen, I began to realise that this puppy love she had always had for me was something else, something stronger. She...she had this way of manipulating things, people. It was a sickness with her although I did not realise it then. And she wanted me; it was as simple as that. I tried to tell her, as gently as I could, that what I felt for her was not of a romantic nature, and when that did not work I stayed away from Casa Pontina for a while. I thought the time would give her a chance to see things from a different perspective, perhaps even meet someone else.'

'But that didn't work either?' Claire asked faintly.

'No, it did not,' he said grimly. 'She started to be wherever I was, then she took to turning up at my home—two, sometimes three times a week.'

'Did you tell Donato?'

'I tried, but he did not understand. Hell, I did not understand! And then Donato's father became ill and he had enough to do to take care of the businesses and run Casa Pontina. I could not burden him with anything else,' Romano said wearily.

She wanted to reach out to him, to touch that harsh, tortured profile with the palm of her hand, to take away the pain that turned the deep voice to gravel. But the knowledge that he didn't love her, that he was still going to say goodbye at the end of all this, stayed her hand. 'And so...?'

'And so one night when I came home late I found a broken window and Bianca in my bed. She had taken an overdose.' She saw his shoulder muscles clench under his shirt at the memory. 'And I decided if she loved me that much I owed it to the rest of the family and Donato to make her happy. I didn't love anyone else, there was no sacrifice involved in that way, and she had been part of my life for a long time. I did not want it to end in tragedy.'

'Did Donato know? About the overdose?' Claire asked softly, trying to imagine how he must have felt.

'No, he still does not know,' Romano said quietly. 'I took her home that night and we announced our engagement, and we married six months later when Bianca was seventeen. Within a month of the marriage I realised I had made a terrible mistake. What I had thought was love on her part was an obsession, a sickness. The things that happened...' He shook his head slowly. 'I would not burden you with the knowledge.'

'And then she discovered that in order to have a child she would need an operation.' He looked at Claire then, his eyes black and bottomless. 'And the sickness really took over. She was frightened to have surgery, and she directed her own fear and hate and resentment at any young woman of childbearing age. Life became a living hell for us both.'

'But Grace must have come into the family about then?' Claire asked hesitantly. 'Bianca didn't...?'

'All that you can imagine and much more besides,' Romano said grimly. 'Of course I did not know about it at the time—Bianca was cunning and Grace kept quiet for the sake of family harmony—but she was the means of separating Donato and Grace after Paolo's death with a pack of lies which continued right up to the day she died.'

'Oh, Romano...' She did touch him then, with light, tentative fingers on his muscled arm, and he gazed down at her small hand on his skin for some moments before he spoke again.

'After her death I found out she had indulged in numerous affairs. I suspected it when she was alive but she was clever and I could never obtain proof. Her obsession with me had long since turned to hate, especially after I made her seek medical help for her instability. Her doctor felt that her condition might well be a hereditary weakness, but as she was adopted it could not be proved one way or the other.'

Claire could hardly take in what he was saying, the bustle and noise all around them distant and unreal as her heart and mind and will focused on the tortured man at her side. And he *was* tortured; she had never seen it so clearly. She wanted to gather him into her arms, to smother his face with kisses, to tell him that it was all right, that she would *make* it all right, but she didn't. She sat quietly, with her hand still on his arm, as his words burnt into her brain.

'She was killed when her car went off the road because she was driving too fast in an effort to get away from being found out at last,' he continued quietly. 'She had arranged a confrontation with Grace that went badly wrong, for Bianca at least. Donato turned up and overheard her admit she had conspired to break up their marriage. I have always been very grateful that Benito sent Donato there. Bianca could be physically violent at times, and who can know what she might have done that day in her rage and fury?'

'Benito?' Claire asked faintly. She knew Grace was overly fond of the parrot and now, for the first time, she understood why.

'*Sì*, Benito. He overheard a telephone conversation and repeated enough for Donato to understand where Grace was and that something was badly wrong,' Romano said grimly.

'I see.' Her mind was buzzing, leaping from one fact

to another as it tried to sort out all it needed to absorb. But one thing was paramount, crystal-clear: *he hadn't loved Bianca*. His marriage had been a nightmare from beginning to end, he had said so, but then why wasn't her heart leaping for joy? Intuition, born of her love for him, knew what was coming next, that was why.

'I do not want emotional commitment, Claire.' He turned fully to face her now, his handsome face white except for a streak of dark colour across the hard cheekbones. 'When Bianca died...it was almost worse than when she had been alive. I felt such guilt, such terrifying guilt, that I could be relieved she had gone. She was young, she had her whole life ahead of her, but the feeling of release from the horror was so intense all I could feel for a long time was a tangle of emotions that woke me in the night in a cold sweat and made me fear for my own sanity.'

'But she was sick.' Claire wasn't aware she had clutched hold of him in her urgency. 'She was ill, Romano, you said so yourself.'

'And I was her husband and responsible for her,' he ground out bitterly. 'For months, years, since the first weeks of our marriage, I had looked into the future and seen a long, dark road that was hell on earth stretching before me. It made the loneliness, the rejection I had endured in my childhood seem like paradise in comparison. But I was her husband. I had made vows to care for her in sickness and health before God and man. There could be no escape.'

'But...but that was different.' She was out of her depth, struggling to put her heart's cry into words, to reach out to him, to help him. 'With Bianca it was different. You would never have that situation again. When you meet someone you can love—'

'I have met someone I can love, Claire.' It was said gently, but with a terrible remoteness that made her flesh go cold. 'I loved you from the first moment I saw you at the airport, with your face lifted up to the sunlight and your hair a blaze of colour in the midst of all the bustle and rush. Oh, I fought the knowledge, of course, every step of the way. Love is an illusion, remember? A mythical prop, propagated by others for their own ends. But all the time I knew I loved you, and then you told me you loved me, so bravely, so courageously...' The black eyes were bitter, his voice flat.

'I wanted to believe what we had was merely a physical attraction, something I have felt for other women and which, once sated, has ceased to be of importance. But when you confessed your love it made me face up to what I have been running away from for months. I love you.'

'Romano...Romano, we can make it work—'

He cut off her feverish entreaties by rising abruptly, the smouldering emotion evident in his glittering eyes and chiselled features immediately banked down at her pleading. 'No—no, we cannot, Claire. I am a coward, you understand this? You look at me and you see a big, strong man, *si*? Someone who is brave, who will fight the dragons? But the last two weeks have made me face that I am a coward. I love you, but I cannot take on the responsibility for another human soul again.'

'You wouldn't have to,' she babbled desperately, rising too and clutching hold of his arms, frightened he would turn and leave before she could make him see. 'It's not like that. I love you and you love me. Everything will work out—'

'No.' He shook his head slowly. 'I cannot bring you into my hell, Claire, the hell that still exists in here.' He tapped the side of his head angrily. 'I was not lying to you when I said I believed love did not exist. Until I met you I felt that way. I had never experienced it, you see, with my parents, with my wife—'

'But Donato and Grace—they love you. And Lorenzo—'

'That is different. They do not really know me—not the Romano deep inside who is not all he should be.' His voice was heartbreakingly sad. 'They see what I present to them.'

'No, no, they don't. You're wrong,' she said urgently. 'We all have secret fears and insecurities, things that wake us in the night sometimes, failings that dog our footsteps. That's why it's so important to have someone to stand in the gap with us, *for us* at times, to love us in spite of ourselves. Your childhood, the terrible time with Bianca—of course they are going to affect you—'

'But I want you to have someone who is strong,' he said, with a flat grimness that frightened her still more. 'You deserve the best.'

'You're strong—don't you see that you're strong?' she said helplessly, knowing she wasn't getting through to him. 'All that you've gone through has given you an insight, a depth of understanding that is far beyond what the average person could have. Oh...' She gazed at him as the handsome face remained stony. 'Stop being so...so *Italian*! I love you—I love you. Doesn't that count for anything?' She flung herself on him, her face awash with tears, beyond caring about anything but the need to make him see. 'You don't have to be macho man all the time.'

He hesitated for one moment, as she pressed herself into him, before crushing her against him so fiercely she felt as though her bones would crack. For a second, a stunningly sweet second, she thought it was going to be all right—and then he pushed her away, holding her gently as he gazed into her swimming eyes, his own wet too. 'I love you too much to let you do this. One day you will see it is for the best,' he said brokenly. 'You want someone young and fresh and wholesome, without any darkness and shadows to mar and destroy. I am old—far, far too old in my head.'

'You don't mean that—you don't.' She twisted in his

hold to get closer to him, but his arms tightened to steel and he continued to hold her at arm's length. 'What about Attilio? He was young and fresh and wholesome, wasn't he? And you didn't want me to have him.'

'I did not say I could stand being around to see it,' he said grimly. 'If I saw another man touch you, hold you...' He shook his head slowly. 'Let us just say that is not possible.'

'Romano, I love you.' She became quiet in his hold, still, her eyes great luminous pools of pain and her face lint-white. 'I can't bear this.'

'Listen to me—listen.' He shook her gently, his eyes mirroring her agony. 'One day you will meet someone else. You are young—you have your whole life before you.' She would have spoken then but he said, 'No, listen to me, Claire. You *will* meet someone else, fall in love, get married, do all the right things. I did not want...I did not want you to go away thinking that it was you, or to allow anything that this Jeff had said to you in the past to continue to haunt you. You are beautiful—incredibly, breathtakingly beautiful. I did not think it was possible for someone to be so beautiful inside and out.'

'But I'm not beautiful enough to make you change your mind,' she said wretchedly, unable to stop the tears coursing down her cheeks. 'That's what you're really saying, isn't it?'

'You will always have my heart, Claire, *always*. I shall never marry and I shall never love again—'

'*Stop it.*' She jerked away from him now so fiercely that she almost overbalanced. 'Do you think that makes it better? *Do you?* Because it doesn't,' she hissed angrily as her temper rose at what he was putting them both through. 'I don't want just your heart, I want you—flesh-and-blood you—every day. I want to see you in the morning when I wake up, be with you at night, make love with you, feed you, laugh with you, have...have your children…' She couldn't speak now, her sobs choking her.

'Goodbye, Claire.' His voice was husky and strained, and as he turned to leave her throat constricted with fear. He was really going to leave. What could she do? God, help me, give me the words, make him see…

'Romano?' She stood there stricken, despair squeezing her heart so tightly she couldn't breathe, and watched him walk out of her life.

CHAPTER ELEVEN

JULY. Claire stared out of the window into the driving rain outside and sighed wearily. No one could believe it was the middle of July; the month had had the worst weather on record. Day after day of torrential rain, sharp winds and it was *cold*. She had even brought her winter jumpers out.

She turned now, surveying her bedroom in the early-morning light that was grey and sombre. Not that she minded really, if she was honest. She felt so bad inside, so wretched, so utterly, utterly hopeless... The tears started and she blinked them away furiously, scrubbing at her face with her hand before walking over to her wardrobe and selecting leggings and a long baggy jumper in bright red, in total defiance of her mood.

The nights were for crying, the days for getting on with life—painful though that was. It was a decision she had made her first night home after that awful journey from Italy, when she had felt she was going mad with pain and grief and rage as she had howled her misery into her mother's ample bosom while her father had forcibly prevented her brothers from getting on the first plane to Italy. She had realised then, after that initial letting down of the floodgates, that for the sake of the rest of the family she had to at least give the appearance of coping with this thing.

It wasn't easy, but she was managing it, and certainly the overwhelmingly generous cheque she had found tucked away in her luggage from Donato and Grace had helped. It meant she wasn't desperate to find an immediate job in England and that she could do something she had wanted to do for a long time: work voluntarily at the home for mentally and physically handicapped children that was situated on the outskirts of the town in Kent where she lived.

She had rung Grace the minute she had found the envelope, protesting that it was too much, that what she had done she had done for love, that she didn't want any payment at all. But when Grace had begun to get upset at her refusal to accept the cheque she had capitulated, and Grace had been thrilled when she'd learnt what the money was indirectly being used for.

So now, as she dressed quickly after a warm shower, fixing her hair into a high ponytail at the back of her head and not bothering with any make-up, she checked that no trace of the tears was left. The children she worked with had problems, enormous problems, and for them she had to be seen to be bright, cheerful and positive, whatever she was feeling like inside. Strangely, when she was with them it wasn't too difficult—her respect and admiration for their bravery in the face of sometimes impossible odds causing her to put her own misery to the back of her mind.

But the nights—the nights were a different matter. Once she was alone in her room, and the rest of the house was sleeping, she lay for hours tossing and turning as she conducted endless post mortems that served no useful purpose at all, and her pillow was always wet when she eventually drifted into a troubled and restless slumber.

Romano loved her, but the prospect of making any pledge, however small, was beyond him. She hadn't demanded a ring on her finger, or vows of undying eternal love, but she had wanted a deep, emotional commitment before getting physically involved with him. She couldn't have coped with the light affair he had wanted at first; she just wasn't made that way. It would have destroyed her, feeling as she did, never to know from one day to the next if their relationship was over, to be unable to ask anything of him, not to have the right to get close.

She had regretted her stand at first through the anguish of the long, lonely, tear-soaked nights, feeling she should have taken anything, *anything* he offered rather than endure this misery. But in the cold light of day, when she examined her heart and the essence of what made her tick, she knew she couldn't have acted any differently.

Loving him as she did, she wouldn't have been able to bear the constant cycle of wild happiness when she was with him, nagging uncertainty when she wasn't, fear that any day he would tell her their relationship was at an end, anger, pain, contempt at her own weakness—oh, everything an affair with him would have involved. No, she had been right to hold out for more, even if that had resulted in his coming to terms with the fact that he loved her and the ultimate decision that had brought him to.

And that was that. Another stage of her life over and finished. The pale, sad-eyed girl in the mirror stared back at her, the expression in the velvety brown eyes belying the valiant stance, and she grimaced in disgust. 'Snap out of it, Claire, you've a job to do so get on with it,' she said aloud. And she was *not* going to wallow in self-pity and despair. She was *not*. Well, only for a bit longer anyway...

The day was hectic but she welcomed the fast pace, the constant challenges, the relentless pushing of mental and physical resources. It gave her less time to brood if every moment was occupied, and it certainly was at Grassacres. But, as always, when she left the big red-brick building and walked down the long pebbled drive bordered on each side by green sweeping lawns, she was so tired she could barely put one foot in front of the other.

Nevertheless she always walked home, Grassacres being just a fifteen-minute stroll from her house, whatever the weather. It gave her a chance to build up a stockpile of determined cheerfulness and resolve for the evening ahead with her family, until she could legitimately escape to the sanctuary of her room and howl her eyes out for what might have been.

As she walked through the big, institution-style iron gates that were constantly left open, and onto the path beyond, her thoughts were on nothing more disturbing than the weather. In strict contrast to the rain and wind of the morning the evening was mellow and quiet, warm, even, with a shy, delicate sun peeping nervously through the clouds and the very English smell of woodsmoke flavouring the air.

It was so pleasant after the torrential rain of the last three weeks that she stood for a second just savouring the air, shutting her eyes and lifting her head to the shaft of sunlight glancing through the big oak tree to her right as she drew on the moment of natural tranquillity.

'Pardon me, but isn't this where I came in?'

She hadn't noticed the big car that had been parked a good way down the street and that at her exit from the home had edged rapidly forwards. But now, as the deep, heavily accented voice met her ears, she went deathly white, turning to face the big, dark man who was leaning out of the window. She stared at him for one endless moment—and then she ran, taking to her heels and flying along the path bordering the walled grounds of Grassacres on one side and the main road on the other, as though her life depended on it.

She heard him call her name but she didn't stop, and then there was the sound of the car engine, a screech of brakes, and a moment or two later a steel hand locked on her arm, stopping the headlong flight and swinging her round to face him.

'Claire?' His voice was wretched now, deep, full of

pain, and as she looked into his face, that dear, dear face she had never expected to see again, she lost the last of what little control she had.

'How could you? How *could* you?' She beat against his chest with her fists as she wailed her anguish out loud, without really knowing what she was railing against. It might have been the desolate vacuum of the last few weeks, the knowledge that she had lost him, that she would never marry, have children, be a half of a whole, or it might even have been just that lazy, assured greeting, when he had spoken as though the nightmare that had been her days and her nights hadn't affected him at all. Whatever, she was hysterical now and he recognised it.

'No more. No more, my love.' He held both her wrists in one hand as he folded her struggling body into the protection of his, his strength eventually subduing her frenzy until she collapsed against him and would have fallen to the ground but for his arms about her. She continued to cry, helplessly and in total abandonment to the torment and suffering she had endured, as he lifted her up into his arms and carried her over to the car, placing her inside as though she were the finest Meissen porcelain.

She shut her eyes and lay back against the seat, utterly exhausted, as he walked swiftly round the bonnet and slid into the car, and then her eyes snapped wide as it suddenly occurred to her what a fright she must look. She had never been able to cry prettily, the way some women could. From a little girl her nose had gone bulbous and red, her skin blotchy, and her eyes gave the impression she had done a few rounds with Mohammed Ali.

'Here.' A large, crisp white handkerchief appeared under her nose in the next moment. 'Blow.'

'I don't want to blow.' It was childish but she had to keep a mental distance from him. She dared not even begin to think, hope, what his presence in England—in her part of England—might mean.

Nevertheless, she knew in the next second or two that her nose was going to behave in a most unladylike fashion, and so she snatched the handkerchief without looking at him, drying her face with the scented linen and then giving her nose the requisite blow.

'Better?'

It was the tender note that did it, that and the fact that she made the mistake of turning her head and looking at him. He looked gorgeous, devastatingly gorgeous, and tired, shattered—haggard, even—but still possessed of the sort of dark hypnotic magnetism that would make a fortune if it could be gift-wrapped.

And, contrary to every sensible, logical, self-protecting principle she had hammered herself with for the last few weeks, she fell against him, her face lifted up to his and her hands going round his neck in a bear hug that would have crushed a lesser man. 'I hate you...' And then his mouth had claimed hers, violently, possessively, ravaging her with a need that exactly matched the burning desire that was consuming her from head to toe.

'Claire, for crying out loud...' It was a low, deep groan, and then she found herself literally lifted back into her seat from lying across his lap. The next moment the car's engine had growled into life and they were moving into the flow of traffic.

'Fasten your seat belt.'

'What?' She stared at him, unable to respond to the terse command as ice froze her limbs.

'I said, fasten your seat belt—and stop looking at me like that, dammit. Did you want me to take you in the front of a hired car with half of the Kent population passing by?' he asked grittily. 'Because in one minute more that's exactly what would have happened.'

'I wouldn't have minded,' she said, with touching honesty.

'Well, your brothers would. I have had two of them breathing down my neck for the last half an hour while I talked to your parents, and it was not something I wish to repeat.' It was said with significant emphasis. 'And I understand the one who is still at work is the biggest of them all.'

'You've been to my home?' she asked incredulously.

'Of course I've been to your home. How do you think I know where you work?' he asked softly, glancing at her for one moment and then swerving violently away from the kerb as his eyes became fixed on her swollen, ravished mouth. 'Hell, you're going to kill us both.'

'*Me?*'

'Yes, you,' he groaned slowly. 'What I want to do to you right at this moment is not conducive to good driving, but I have to get to where other people are to talk to you. I cannot trust myself if we are alone, and I have to explain without touching you...'

'But why do we need other people?' she asked dazedly, and then, as she glanced down, the state of his body provided the answer. His arousal was hot and fierce. 'Oh...'

'Yes, oh,' he agreed grimly, not looking at her now. But she didn't mind—oh, she didn't, she didn't, she didn't. Because it was going to be all right, however grim and controlled and austere he appeared right now. He had come for her, hadn't he? Braved her parents, her brothers, and come to seek her out. It had to be all right...didn't it?

It did. He parked right in the middle of the town at the edge of the market square, which was still full of mums and tots sitting by the fountain, commuters having a break in the sunshine before their journey home, shoppers, and the inevitable courting couples sitting close on the wooden slatted seats.

'I love you, Claire, and I cannot let you go.' It was said without any preamble, but as she turned to him again he opened his door and got out, walking round to her side and drawing her out of the car with a shake of his head. 'Out, wench,' he said wryly, 'I need to talk to you, to explain, to…to ask your forgiveness. And one more minute in that car and all these little children are going to have a firsthand demonstration of the facts of life.'

'Romano…' But he drew her over to a vacant seat, with just a few pigeons pecking desultorily at the crumbs of a broken ice-cream cornet as their audience.

'I cannot live without you at my side, Claire.' She stared at him, stilled by the desperate note in his voice that had wiped away any amusement or lightness. 'But it will not be easy. You have to understand this—understand what you would be taking on if you want me. It is not right, it is not fair that I ask you to marry me like this—you are warmth and light and purity and I…I am dark, here, in the heart of me.'

'You are asking me to marry you?' she asked stupidly, her senses drinking in the closeness of him, the smell, the sheer sensual power, even as her mind refused to co-operate with any coherent instructions.

'You once said to me that you would not let the past beat you—you remember this?' he asked huskily.

She shook her head numbly, her mind refusing to concentrate on anything but the fact, the glorious, wonderful, amazing fact, that he wanted to *marry* her.

'*Sì*, you did, and it hit me like the…the nail from the blue?'

'A bolt from the blue,' she corrected him dazedly, her eyes drinking in the sheer beauty of him.

'Ah, yes, the bolt. And that was because for the last three years the past has beaten me, held me, ground me into the dust. I did not want to acknowledge it, but it is true. And then, when I met you, when I fell instantly

and terribly in love, the past was there in all its blackness, telling me that this would not work either, that you
could not be what you seemed, that even if you were it
would all turn to ashes given time. And so I played the
coward—'

'No—no, you didn't. You were trying to be honest—'

'I played the coward, Claire.' He interrupted her quick
and fervent protest with an upraised hand and a crooked,
pained smile that smote at her heart. 'I thought I could
get through. I told myself it was not right to inflict my
nightmares on you—I still think that. But the fact of the
matter is...I am useless without you in my life. I have
not slept, eaten; I have been unable to work—and then
I realised that I would rather be a coward with you than
without you. If you still wanted me, that is. I faced the
fact that I might have driven you away for good and sent
myself half-mad in the process.'

'You couldn't drive me away,' she said simply.
'Where could I go that I didn't carry you with me in my
heart?'

'I do not deserve you, and I will be hell to live with—
you understand this? The years of my boyhood, the time
with Bianca—I cannot easily express what I feel. I am
bound, deep inside.'

'I'll release you.' She moved closer to him now, lifting her arms up round his neck but without any pressure,
resting against him as she spoke into his throat. 'Do you
hear me? I'll release you.'

'And I will be jealous. I know this. When I saw Attilio
with his hands on you—' He stopped abruptly. 'I could
have ripped him apart, limb by limb,' he groaned huskily. 'Can you cope with a man like this?'

'All my life.' She nuzzled into his throat now, licking
his skin with a delicate, tentative tongue, and immediately his arms came round her and he crushed her to
him.

'But I will love you, Claire, this I can promise,' he

said hoarsely. 'I will love you for eternity. There will never be anyone else. You will be the air I breathe, my sun, moon and stars, my wife, the mother of my children, the other half of me. I will love you, want you, every day, every moment. Hell, I could eat you alive...'

And as the pigeons flew in a startled arc into the evening air, surprised and not a little shocked at the passions that afflicted these strange human creatures, he gathered her up into his arms, his mouth hot and sensuous on hers as he carried her back to the car, and to the beginning of his walk out of the shadows and into the glorious light of love.

From national
bestselling author

SHARON
SALA

SWEET BABY

So many secrets...

It happened so long ago that Tory Lancaster can't
recall being the little girl who came home to an
empty house.

A woman now, Tory is trying to leave behind the
scarring emotions of abandonment and sorrow—
desperate to love, but forever afraid to trust. With the
help of a man who claims to love her, Tory is able to
meet the past head-on—a past haunted by images of
a mysterious tattooed man and the doll that was her
only friend. But there are so many secrets, so
little time....

Available in February 1998
at your favorite retail outlet.

**The Brightest Stars
in Women's Fiction™**

MIRA

Don't miss these Harlequin favorites by some of our top-selling authors!

HT#25733	THE GETAWAY BRIDE	$3.50 U.S. ☐	
	by Gina Wilkins	$3.99 CAN. ☐	
HP#11849	A KISS TO REMEMBER	$3.50 U.S. ☐	
	by Miranda Lee	$3.99 CAN. ☐	
HR#03431	BRINGING UP BABIES	$3.25 U.S. ☐	
	by Emma Goldrick	$3.75 CAN. ☐	
HS#70723	SIDE EFFECTS	$3.99 U.S. ☐	
	by Bobby Hutchinson	$4.50 CAN. ☐	
HI#22377	CISCO'S WOMAN	$3.75 U.S. ☐	
	by Aimée Thurlo	$4.25 CAN. ☐	
HAR#16666	ELISE & THE HOTSHOT LAWYER	$3.75 U.S. ☐	
	by Emily Dalton	$4.25 CAN. ☐	
HH#28949	RAVEN'S VOW	$4.99 U.S. ☐	
	by Gayle Wilson	$5.99 CAN. ☐	

(limited quantities available on certain titles)

AMOUNT	$ _____
POSTAGE & HANDLING	$ _____
($1.00 for one book, 50¢ for each additional)	
APPLICABLE TAXES*	$ _____
TOTAL PAYABLE	$ _____

(check or money order—please do not send cash)

To order, complete this form and send it, along with a check or money order for the total above, payable to Harlequin Books, to: **In the U.S.:** 3010 Walden Avenue, P.O. Box 9047, Buffalo, NY 14269-9047; **In Canada:** P.O. Box 613, Fort Erie, Ontario, L2A 5X3.

Name: _____

Address: _____ City: _____

State/Prov.: _____ Zip/Postal Code: _____

Account Number (if applicable): _____

*New York residents remit applicable sales taxes.
Canadian residents remit applicable GST and provincial taxes.

Look us up on-line at: http://www.romance.net

075-CSAS

HBLJM98